FROSTBITE

7-10-02.
To Daren

FROSTBITE

NATHAN GRAZIANO

GREEN BEAN PRESS
NEW YORK, NEW YORK
2002

Green Bean Press
P.O. Box 237
New York, NY 10013 USA
718-302-1955 ph/fax
gbpress@earthlink.net

ISBN 1-891408-26-7
Library of Congress Control Number: 2001098408

DISCLAIMER:

The following is a work of fiction. Although the settings are real, the characters and events are entirely made up. Any similarity to any persons, living or dead, is purely coincidental.

ACKNOWLEDGEMENTS

The author would like to thank the editors of the journals where sections of this book originally appeared.

Also, 4 lines of a Ramones song are reprinted on page 112. The author and publisher would like to thank the band and their lawyers for paying no attention to that whatsoever.

For a complete list of titles published by Green Bean Press, as well as information about upcoming projects, special deals, free downloads and other cool stuff, visit us online.
http://www.greenbeanpress.com

for my mother

TABLE OF CONTENTS

We live, as we dream—alone....

—Joseph Conrad,
Heart of Darkness

PADLOCKED

I'm staring at the ceiling with a bloody sock pressed to my forehead. A nurse with deep wrinkles and jowls peers up at me over her glasses. She takes a deep breath, opens her mouth as if she's going to say something, shakes her head and looks down at the computer screen.

Ryan gives me the middle finger through a window separating the check-in office from the corridor. The nurse looks up and sees him. Shakes her head again.

"Is he your friend?" she asks, seemingly unimpressed with Ryan's ability to shoot the double-bird while touching his tongue to his nose.

"My roommate," I say and shrug.

"Please tell him to stay in the waiting room," she says, nodding in his direction and rolling her eyes at me.

I stick my head out the door. "Hey, go back to the waiting room, man," I say to Ryan.

"Oh, sorry," he says. As he turns around, he sticks his ass out at me and slaps his butt cheeks. I hear the nurse sigh behind me.

"What's your name?" She doesn't look up from the computer screen.

"Russ Fuller. F-U-L-L-E-R."

"Date of birth?"

"4-28-78."

"Address?"

I tell her my address and she types it into the computer. A thin stream of blood trickles down my face and onto my shirt.

"Excuse me, but do you think—"

The nurse looks at the blood, shakes her head and, slowly, as if it's a great effort, gets up from her chair. "I'll get you a towel and some ice," she says. And shakes her head. Again.

As soon as she leaves the office, Ryan comes back. He's standing in the middle of the corridor playing the air guitar, doing one of those Pete Townshend windmill strums with his arm. I laugh. The old nurse walks up behind Ryan and taps him on the shoulder. I see her pointing to the waiting room with one hand and shaking her finger at him with the other.

As soon as she turns around, he gives her the single-bird and grabs his crotch with the other hand. She comes back into the room, mumbling to herself. She's one of those people whose mouth seems to be stuck frowning. The only way for her to crack a smile would be to stand on her head.

She hands me a white washcloth. "Thank you," I say.

"That's your roommate? How old is he?" Without waiting for my reply, she says, "He acts like a five year old." She sits back down in front of the computer screen.

"He's 22," I say. She's not listening.

"I don't know what's wrong with you college kids," she says.

"Well, actually, we're both graduating on Saturday," I say.

She doesn't respond. Just shakes her head.

After the guy we lived with junior year failed out, Ryan and I needed to find a roommate to rent out the third bedroom in our apartment. We put flyers in the Union Building, on some of the buildings in downtown Plymouth, all around campus. The place wasn't much to look at. It was an old house, divided into four separate overpriced apartments. One of the pluses, though, was that with the paper-thin walls on the second floor, we could hear all the juicy sex conversations of the sorority girls who lived next to us. Some nights we could even hear them getting laid. We figured we had a marketable place. Within a week Rich Mayo called.

Rich came over on a Thursday afternoon before finals week.

When I answered the door and stared down at him, I was convinced that he'd been orphaned from the Lollipop Guild in *The Wizard Of Oz*. That was around the same time we discovered that the movie matched up perfectly with *Dark Side Of The Moon* if you started the CD on the lion's third roar, so the image of those dwarves dancing to "Us and Them" was still crisp in my mind. Rich stood in the doorway, flexing his neck. He wore a white tank top with *Hampton Beach* written across the front. He had a very muscular upper body. But his legs were these little stumps, no longer than my forearm. And his face and shoulders and back were covered with these large, bulbous zits and acne patches.

"I'm Rich Mayo," he said.

"Come on in," I said, "I'm Russ." I lead him down the hallway into the living room. When Rich walked in, Ryan's eyes widened. He stood up to shake Rich's hand, smiling uncomfortably. Rich had one of those vise-grip handshakes that nearly snapped off your fingers.

"Good to meet you. I'm Rich Mayo," he said to Ryan, flexing his chest. He had a high voice which cracked on stressed syllables.

"Would you like a beer?" I asked, sitting down next to Ryan on the couch. The couch was literally on its last leg; the other three legs had been broken off, and old biology textbooks propped it up.

"No, thanks. I'm training," Rich said, rolling his neck.

"Oh," I said, looking at Ryan.

"Well, would you like the big tour?" Ryan asked.

Rich cracked his knuckles. "In a second," he said.

"You can sit down if you'd like," I said, pointing to a chair across from us. I couldn't stop looking at his tiny legs and full-sized ass in the pair of loose-fitting jeans he was wearing. I thought about the alterations that must've had to have been made to his pants. It was freaky. I wanted him to sit.

"Nah, I'll stand. I've been sitting in class all day," he said, looking around. "This is a pretty nice place. But I guess it won't really matter that much. I just need a place to stay during the week. I go home to Hampton on weekends."

I looked at Ryan, who nodded his head. Someone who would

pay rent but not stick around on weekends? I nodded back to him. Perfect.

We showed Rich the apartment—the tub lined with a layer of grime, the old faucets with rust around the nozzles, the dishes stacked and growing mold in the kitchen sink. Rich kept flexing his chest and shoulders, rolling his neck. I walked behind him, watching those legs. When we told him about the sorority girls in the next apartment, he clapped his hands together. For the first time, he seemed enthused. One of the zits on his forehead was on the brink of bursting.

"Really! That's very nice. Very nice," he said.

"Sometimes," Ryan said, "you can hear them masturbate."

"Yeah! Yeah! Yeah!" Rich continued clapping.

The next afternoon the three of us drove down to the landlord's office and signed a new lease.

The nurse takes the blood-pressure cuff off my left arm and shakes her head. Her beady eyes keep peering at me over the reading glasses. "140 over 92," she says. "That's high for a young man."

"I know, " I say, "it runs in my family."

"Are you a smoker?" she asks.

"Yes."

"You should quit now, or you're going to be a prime candidate for a heart attack," she says and grabs my wrist to check my pulse.

Combine my blood pressure with the stress of graduating on Saturday, and I'll be lucky if I don't drop dead of a major coronary by the end of tonight. It seems that everyone—even Ryan, who's in the waiting room putting the moves on a girl hunched over, clutching her gut—has something lined up after graduation. It seems like everyone has an idea of what they're going to do with their lives. They have direction and answers. Me? Shit. I'm going to continue cooking at a restaurant up in Waterville Valley, dusting the frame on my degree with the same dishrags I use at work.

"82," the nurse says, and types my vital signs into the computer. "So what exactly happened to you again?"

Rich moved in the last week of August. He drove into town pulling a small U-Haul latched to the back bumper of his blue Ford Tempo. Ryan and I were sitting on the couch watching television while Rich brought his stuff in. We asked him if he wanted help unpacking, but he just shook his head and grunted. He carried in three big cardboard boxes, a mattress, an old recliner, a television and a small refrigerator. He closed his bedroom door each time he went outside to get something else, like there was something in his bedroom that we weren't supposed to see.

After he moved in, he always kept his bedroom door shut. He actually went to the hardware store and bought a padlock. Whenever he left the apartment the padlock was on. The room became a mystery that stirred my imagination.

He also had some strange habits. For example, he seemed to survive solely on hot dogs, ketchup and pasta mixed together. We didn't know if he kept different foods in the refrigerator he'd brought into his room when he moved in, but I did see him eat the hot dog/ketchup/pasta meal at least twice a day.

The strangest thing about him, though, by far, was the fact that he was almost always playing the air guitar. Any time I saw him he was either in the middle of an intense solo or casually strumming a rhythm. One time I even saw him jump fretboards on the invisible version of the old Jimmy Page signature double-neck. To my knowledge, he didn't own an *actual* guitar; but he did have an arsenal of air distortion petals, air amplifiers, air picks, air finger slides. And the most remarkable thing about his air guitar was the fact that he didn't need background music to play it. The music apparently played in his head.

As the first semester living with Rich ended, and his performances reached well into the hundreds, I knew, inevitably, I'd have to ask him about his air guitar.

The nurse hands me a towel packed with ice and tells me to go back to the waiting room until my name is called.

I take a seat next to Ryan, who is still talking with the girl clutching her stomach and groaning.

"I'm telling you, baby, you just ate something bad," he says, poking his elbow at my ribs. "Russ, this is Stephanie. Stephanie, this is the guy I was telling you about."

I extend out my hand to Stephanie, a cute brunette with short hair and a pierced eyebrow.

"Good to meet you, Stephanie," I say.

"Nice to meet...ugh...you, too," Stephanie says, weakly shaking my hand.

"Oh, Jesus, I'm such an asshole. Russ, this is Stephanie's friend, Alicia," Ryan says pointing his thumb towards an overweight girl flipping through a copy of *People*.

"Nice to meet you, Alicia," I say. She waves without looking up from the magazine.

"So what did they tell you?" Ryan asks, rubbing Stephanie's back as she groans.

"I have to wait for a doctor, like the rest of them," I say, shaking my head at him. He smiles. The man never quits.

"So what does the nurse think?" he says. Stephanie clutches her stomach tighter and groans. "It's all right, baby. I'm sure it's nothing serious."

"She said I'll probably need a couple of stitches. Man, this really turned out to be a bust," I say.

"Yeah, but now you *know*, man," he says, smiling as he continues to rub small circles on Stephanie's back. "I'm sure it's just something you ate, sweetie."

By mid-March, there was still close to a foot of snow on the ground in Plymouth. I only had two months until graduation. Time was an issue. I decided to finally talk to Rich about the air guitar, after close to six months of ignoring it. I needed some answers.

I came home from class on a cold Tuesday afternoon. Rich's door was closed, but not padlocked. I walked into the kitchen. He was standing in front of the stove, waiting for a pot of water to boil. He had the hot dogs, ketchup and a box of ziti on the counter.

His head was down, and his tongue was half out of his mouth. He moved his hand down the fretboard, stopping toward the bottom and furiously finger-tapping licks like Eddie Van Halen. His face was red.

I didn't want to interrupt him in the middle of a solo.

I stood in the doorway of the kitchen, scratching the back of my neck. I coughed. Rich ignored me and continued. Then he spun in a circle, kicked his leg out, jumped in the air, and fell to his knees, bending the last note. When the song was over, he kept his head down, and, with both hands over his head, made the Van Halen sign with his fingers.

"Hey, Rich," I said.

Rich stood up. "Hey. How's it going?"

"Not bad. Not bad. So," I said, pointing to the floor, "what was that you were just playing?"

"What are you talking about?" he asked, laughing dryly.

I shrugged. "You know. With the spin thing and the kick in the air. The Van Halen sign. I mean, was it a Van Halen tune? 'Eruption' or maybe 'Mean Street'? "

He laughed again, picked up the box of ziti from the counter and poured it in the boiling water. "*What* are you *talking* about?"

I threw my arms up. "Your solo," I said. "The air guitar."

"I don't know what you're talking about," he said, stirring the pasta with a fork. Then he put down the fork and started strumming a few chords.

"See!" I pointed at his hands. I was getting worked up.

"What are you talking about?" He shrugged and turned his back to me. I could see his arms holding the air guitar.

"The air guitar! You keep playing the air guitar! You were doing it when I walked into the room. And you're doing it now!" I practically shouted.

"You're really messed up. You know that?" he said, turning around and tossing his air pick at me.

"No, man. You're the one who's fucked up!"

With his chest sticking out and fists clenched, he came barreling at me. His head bumped my ribs.

"What did you call me?" he said, staring up at me with his bottom lip trembling.

"I said you're fucked up. You keep playing that air guitar then denying it. You play the fucking thing every time I see you outside of that room! And that, on its own, is fucked up! But now that you're denying it—"

He shoved me against the wall. "You better shut your damn mouth or we're going to have trouble," he said, poking his index finger into my chest.

I looked down at him. The acne on his forehead seemed on the brink of explosion. "Don't fucking push me," I said.

He growled. I shook my head and slowly backed out of the room. Just before I turned my back to walk away, he strummed a chord and held up a fist at me.

I went into my bedroom and sat down on my bed. I reached in my pocket and grabbed a cigarette. I still knew nothing about Rich Mayo and had less than two months to find out. My next step was obvious: I'd have to break into the room.

"So you were at a friend's dorm room when your stomach started to hurt? Hmm…I'm trying to think what that could be. Does it hurt here?" Ryan reaches down and gently places his hand on Stephanie's stomach.

She shakes her head as Alicia looks up from the magazine and rolls her eyes.

If there's one thing I can say about Ryan, it's that he never gives up, which is partly how he landed himself a decent-paying job in Portsmouth. He's moving out on Monday into an apartment in Dover.

"How about this?" Ryan asks. He's just about to reach for a spot closer to her breast, when the nurse appears, shaking her head. "Stephanie Olsen," she says.

Stephanie stands up, tries to smile at Ryan, but groans instead.

"You'll be all right, sweetie. Hey, do you think I can get your number before you leave?"

Stephanie ignores him and follows the nurse through the door into the emergency room. I look at Ryan. I open my mouth and start to say something.

"Russ Fuller."

It's another nurse's voice. She's holding the door open. She's younger, with small features and short blond hair pinned back behind her ears. Cute. Ryan looks at her and smiles. "He's right here, darling," he says.

The nurse smiles back at him.

I get up from the chair, still pressing the towel against my forehead. The ice is starting to melt and drip onto my shirt. I walk towards the door.

"Good luck, buddy," Ryan calls to me. "If you need me to come with you, you just let me know. No, why don't you have this lovely nurse come and get me?"

I follow her inside.

       I bribed Ryan with free beers to go to Biederman's with me to discuss my plan. The pub was empty with the exception of two townies slugging Budweiser drafts and watching candlepin bowling with their stools turned towards a big-screen television in the corner. Ryan and I ordered a couple of Newcastles. I lit a cigarette.

"So here's what I have in mind," I said.

"I can't believe he denied it. That's just fucked up. Like some *Twilight Zone* shit or something," he said.

"Yeah, I know. And I can't believe the little bastard pushed me."

"No shit. You should've clocked him. I mean, he's like two feet tall. You can't be afraid of him."

I shrugged. "I just didn't think of it," I said.

"Hey, look who's coming in." He motioned toward the entrance with his head. "You remember her? It's that chick I nailed our sophomore year. You know, the one who made the pig noises while I was banging her. Remember I told you about that? 'Oh, oh…oink. Squaw, squaw." He laughed, staring at her.

The girl, an attractive redhead, spotted him, turned around and walked out.

"Bye-bye, Wendy," he said, waving with his fingers.

"Jesus Christ, man, will you listen to me?" I said, and punched him in the arm.

"Yeah, I'm sorry. Go on."

I took a long pull from my beer and slammed it down on the bar. "Here it is. We need to break into the room," I said. Ryan shook his head.

"We can get arrested for that shit. If his room is padlocked, we can't just break in."

"No. I know that," I said. "What I was thinking is we'll wait until finals week. I've looked at the lock—all it is is a latch screwed into the wall. All we need to do is get a Phillips head, take the latch off the wall and screw it back on when we're finished. *Voilà.* We're in the room."

"Why is this such a big fucking deal to you?"

I stared him straight in the eyes. "Haven't you ever wondered what's in there? Haven't you ever wondered what the hell this guy's hiding? Don't you think it's slightly fucked up that we've lived with the guy for almost a year and have never seen the inside of that room? This goes beyond morbid curiosity. I'm talking about answers, man."

"You know," he said, shaking his head, "I think you're just as whacked as he is. What's the big deal? The guy pays rent. Does his own thing—albeit a slightly *different* thing—but he doesn't want to be bothered. He does his dishes, goes home on weekends...shit, Russ. He's a perfect roommate."

"But it's more than that!" Trying to articulate to him *why* the answers were so important, it occurred to me, for the first time, that maybe this whole thing wasn't about Rich at all.

"So why does it have to be the last week of school?" Ryan asked.

"Just in case he notices something and flips out. I'm telling you, man, the plan is infallible. We just need to find out when his last exam is and when he's going home. Then, we're golden. A couple turns of a screw, and we're in. What do you say?" I leaned on my elbows, pressing my face close to his.

"I guess so, man. I mean, it's not really a big deal to me, but if you're so bent on it, I'll check it out with you," he said.

I slapped my hand down on the bar. "Nice! Fucking nice! We have two weeks, my man. Cheers." I lifted my glass.

Ryan lifted his indifferently and toasted.

"Yeah, that chick, Wendy, she was good-looking and a pretty nice lay and all, but I just couldn't get over those noises," he said, and made barnyard noises while thrusting his hips against the bar.

I slugged down the rest of my beer and ordered another. The townies continued to watch bowling. One of the bowlers was going for a perfect game. They thought that was incredible. I guess it was.

The young nurse leads me into a curtained cubicle. There's a bed with plain white sheets and a plastic chair beside it. Everything is white.

"You can take a seat on the bed, and the doctor will be with you as soon as possible," she says and leaves, closing the curtain in front of me.

I sit down on the edge of the bed and stare at the ceiling when I hear these low, agonizing moans from the other side of the curtain. It's an older man's voice.

"Ooh ... ooh. I'm dying. Ooh ... ugh. I'm dying. Doctor? Get a doctor, I'm dying."

I try to block it out, leave it to the professionals with medicine and answers.

"Doctor, I'm dying. Somebody get a priest." He starts gasping, choking on his own breath.

"Hey, are you all right in there?" I whisper through the curtain.

"Do I sound all right? I'm dying," the voice says.

"Should I get a doctor?"

"Get a priest. A *priest*."

I panic. Suddenly, everything seems trivialized by the urgency of this thing. Thinking I'm about to have my first real encounter with death, about to hear the sound of life being sucked from the lungs of a man no more than three feet away, I throw open the curtain. I happen to catch the young nurse walking by with x-rays in her hand. I grab her by the elbow.

"Nurse, the man next to me needs help. Quickly. He's dying." I can feel my own heart pounding against my chest. Urgency.

The nurse smiles and places her hand on my shoulder. "Oh, that's just Mr. Sellers. He dropped a gallon of milk on his toe earlier tonight. He may've broken his toe, but we're pretty sure he's not dying," she says and walks away.

I sit back down on the bed and close the curtain. I pick up the towel wrapped with fresh ice and place it against my forehead.

"Did you find a priest?" The voice is weak, brittle.

"No. Sorry, there are no priests available right now," I say.

"But I'm *dying*. I need a Catholic priest."

"Say a prayer."

This afternoon, Rich jumped into his car after finishing his last exam and drove home for the weekend. He told us he was coming on Monday to take his stuff home for the summer. The door to his room was shut. Padlocked. Standing at the window, I watched his car disappear down Langdon Street.

Ryan was sitting on the couch, flipping through a textbook and his notes for his Economics final tomorrow. I finished my last exam yesterday. I haven't started packing. I don't need to be out of the apartment until Tuesday. I stood in front of Ryan, smiling.

"Tonight's the night," I said.

Ryan looked up. "You have a date?"

"No, asshole. Tonight's the night we open the room."

"All right, you want to do it now? I have to study for this exam."

I shook my head. "No, let's wait. You can finish studying. I've waited long enough. Another couple of hours won't kill me. Besides, this isn't something I want to rush into. I need to prepare myself." I rubbed my hands together and laughed.

"Whatever," Ryan said. "You're fucking crazy. You know that? This has become unhealthy. I'm willing to bet there's nothing but a bed, a dresser, a small refrigerator and a television. That's it.

You've been working yourself up over nothing."

I admit, seeing the inside of Rich's room had preoccupied me for much of the semester. Some nights I'd lay awake in bed thinking about the possibilities. Then I'd close my eyes and visualize the room. I tried picturing the interior using fragments of what I remembered before Rich moved in. I imagined pictures of serial killers, Nazi flags, pin-up posters from fetish magazines on the walls—women's feet, gay porn, breast milk squirting—a copy of *The Anarchist's Cookbook* under his bed and small plastic pipe bombs in his closet. Okay, Ryan was right. I was obsessed.

I spent the rest of the afternoon in my bedroom, stabbing my pillow with a Phillips head. I tried taking a nap. I couldn't sleep. At 6:08 p.m. I opened my bedroom door and walked into the living room.

Ryan was watching TV.

"Are you ready?" I asked.

Ryan looked up at me over his shoulder. "You're scaring me, man."

I held up the screwdriver and started to giggle. Ryan stood up from the couch. We walked over to Rich's door. My hands were sweating. I looked at Ryan, unable to speak. I inserted the screwdriver into the hinge on the side of the door and turned. The first screw came out. I handed it to Ryan, then worked out the second screw. I took a deep breath, dug the screwdriver in again. The third. The hinge fell from the wall. The padlock dangled there. Ryan laughed. I placed my hand on the doorknob, took a deep breath and turned.

Inside there was a mattress without sheets and a crumpled red comforter on the end. The walls were bare. The tattered brown recliner sat in front of the small television set, propped up on a milk crate, with a VCR on the floor beside it. Next to the television was the refrigerator. Soiled laundry was scattered on the worn blue rug. I turned to Ryan and shrugged.

Ryan threw up his arms. "See, I told you."

I flung open the refrigerator door. Empty. It seemed the mystery of Rich Mayo would never produce answers; I'd been foolish to think it would. I plopped down on the chair and placed my head in my hands.

"I'm sorry, man," Ryan said, patting me on the back. "I know you were expecting something better."

I looked down at my feet and saw a videotape underneath the chair. I reached down and felt a stack of them. I squealed.

"Wow, you just sounded like Wendy," Ryan said.

"Dude, look at this," I said breathlessly, pulling out one of the videotapes, then another and another.

"Big deal," Ryan said. "He has movies. Who cares?"

"No, these *aren't labeled*," I said, turning on the television and putting one of the tapes in the VCR. Ryan sat down on the floor beside me. We were both silent.

On the television, there was a typical middle-class family room—a couch, a coffee table, a painting of a lake on the wall. Click. Someone behind the camera started a tape on a cassette deck. A keyboard played in the background.

"That's 'Baba O'Riley'," Ryan said, more to himself than me. His eyes never left the screen.

Just before Pete Townshend's guitar kicked in, Rich Mayo jumped into the frame. He wasn't wearing a shirt, only a pair of spandex biker shorts that came down past his knees. With the first chord, Rich struck down powerfully on his air guitar. He had his eyes closed. He stuck his tongue out. He jumped onto the couch then back off, kicking his leg in the air.

"What the fuck?" Ryan said without turning to look at me.

"I don't know, man," I said, shaking my head. "I really don't know what to make of this. I mean, this is unbelievable."

We looked away from the television just as "Baba O'Riley" stopped and the introduction to "Magic Carpet Ride" began. We slowly turned our heads and looked at each other with our mouths open. Then burst into laughter.

A tall, lanky man opens the curtain. He has a long forehead, a receding hairline and a thin, pointed nose. He's wearing a doctor's coat with a stethoscope wrapped around his neck.

He looks down at a clipboard.

"Hello there, Russ. I'm Dr. Stone," he says, extending his hand, but not looking up from the clipboard.

I shake his hand. "Good to meet you," I say.

"Is that a doctor in there? Tell him I need a priest," the voice behind the curtain calls.

"The nurse will be right in with some painkillers, Mr. Sellers. Sit tight," Dr. Stone says, still without looking up from the clipboard. "Hmm. Your blood pressure is a little high for someone your age. You may want to watch that."

He finally looks at me. I look down at the floor. I know what's coming next.

"You may want to think about giving up the cigarettes while you still can," he says.

I nod my head, grateful for the abridged version.

"Let's have a look at this cut," he says and pulls a pair of rubber gloves from the pocket of his doctor's coat. He puts a finger on each side of the cut and stares at it, squinting and nodding his head. "Yeah, that's a good gash. We'll have to put a couple of stitches in."

I start thinking about graduation and black stitches in the photo of me shaking hands with the president of the college.

"How many?" I ask.

"Oh, not too many. Three or four. It's just a really deep one. How did you do that anyway? Bar brawling? Fight with your girlfriend?"

"Something like that," I say.

The front door slammed. I stopped the VCR and ejected the tape. We could hear footsteps approach from the living room. Rich Mayo's stumpy shadow loomed over us. We looked up. He noticed the stack of tapes at my feet. His face turned a deep crimson. A pimple on his forehead oozed. He balled his small hands into fists.

"What the hell are you two doing?" His voice cracked with anger.

Ryan stood up. "We just needed to get into your room to see if there was a power box in here or—"

"My tapes! What are you doing watching my tapes? You fucking assholes!" He pushed Ryan aside with a swipe of his arm and pounced on his tapes, trying to gather them into his arms. I stood up from the chair, grabbed the tape out of the VCR and tried to hand it to him.

"You!" he said, looking up at me. His nostrils flared, and the veins in his neck protruded.

"Listen, I'm sorry, Rich. We really didn't mean to invade your privacy, but we got in here and thought you had porno flicks—"

Smack!

He hit me in the side of my head with one of the tapes. I stumbled back against the television, knocking it off the milk crate. I was stunned. I put my hand to my head, pulled it away and looked at it. My entire palm was covered in blood.

"Oh shit," I said. I could feel the blood start to trickle down my face.

Ryan looked at me. "Oh shit!" he said.

Rich looked at the tape in his hand then the gash on my forehead. His eyes widened. He gathered his tapes in his arms, pushed his way past Ryan and scurried out of the room, calling over his shoulder, "You assholes!"

Ryan stared at me with his mouth open.

"Get me a towel or something, man. I'm bleeding bad!" I pressed my hand against the wound, trying to keep it from gushing all over the rug.

Ryan took off his sock. "Here, use this. I'll get my keys," he said.

I took his nasty sock and pressed it against the cut. As he looked for his car keys, I went into the bathroom and tried to wash some of the blood off my face.

Dr. Stone comes back in with the young nurse carrying a metal tray with a needle, some antiseptic pads, thread, and tweezers. The nurse, already wearing rubber gloves, takes a wet cloth and washes the cut.

"So you're a college student, huh?" Dr. Stone says, placing another pair of plastic gloves on his hands. They make a slapping sound against his skin.

"Actually, I *was* a college student. I'm graduating on Saturday."

"Really? Congratulations. So what did you study?" Dr. Stone says. The nurse dabs the wound with an antiseptic pad. I flinch.

"History," I say, taking a deep breath.

"Really. Any idea what you want to do?" He prepares to stick a needle into my forehead.

"No," I say, closing my eyes, "not really."

BOTTOMS UP

A SKINNY girl with spiked red hair and small silver hoops in her nose, lip and eyebrow, passes the hat to me. It's one of many baseball hats in the kitchen, although the rest are being worn. Mostly backwards. And they all look the same, like they've been dropped in mud and run over by 18-wheelers. I have long hair and don't wear baseball hats. Just a ponytail. But I'm not one of those dirty hippies you see at the bars downtown. The ones who smell like patchouli oil covering up B.O., spin in circles in front of the band at shows and make these weird tai chi movements with their hands.

I reach in my wallet and pull out a buck. I put it in the hat and pass it to the guy standing next to me, wearing a sweatshirt with Sigma Phi's letters. He's also wearing a baseball hat. Backwards, of course.

The hat goes around the kitchen, everyone chipping in a buck or two. It's crowded, hot and smoky. Downstairs, I hear the music blaring from the basement. The basement is also packed with college students. And smoky as hell. For a second, I wonder why I'm even here. Then I remember: Michelle, this cute waitress from work, asked me if I wanted to go to a party. Well, I'm only human.

The hat stops at Quimby, the only other guy in the room not wearing a hat. I've seen him at parties before. He's the chapter president of Sigma Phi, good-looking and as charming as a fucking prince. He looks a little like Kevin Costner, now that I think about it. And the girls are draped around him, nodding and smiling and sticking their chests out at him. He begins counting the money in front of this poor bastard, Scooter. At any frat party there will inevitably be a guy named Scooter. Scooter is stupid drunk and just about falling out of his chair at the kitchen table. His baseball hat is pulled down far over his eyes, and his face is whiter than a raped sheet. He keeps opening and closing his mouth, swallowing his spit.

Eighty-seven dollars, Quimby says, putting the pile of cash on the table in front of Scooter. It's all yours if you down the shot. What do you say, buddy?

About ten minutes earlier, Scooter did a shot of Jeigermeister and immediately went green around the gills. His face cringed up like he was sucking on a lemon. Before he could get to the sink, a mouthful of spew sprayed the table and, among other things, happened to fill a shot glass halfway.

Eighty-seven bucks will buy you a lot of beer, my man. And it's not like you're drinking someone else's puke. It's your own. It won't hurt you, Quimby says, placing his hand on Scooter's back.

And Susie just said she'll show you her tits if you drink it, Scoot. Right, Susie? says this other guy. I think his name is Jay. He has a thick black goatee and wears a baseball hat. Backwards. He puts his arm around a really cute brunette with hair almost down to her ass. She has on a tight red shirt and snug-fitting blue jeans. This would definitely be an incentive if I were into that sort of thing. Drinking my own puke, that is.

Susie nods her head up and down like it's attached to her neck by a hinge.

Scooter takes a deep breath. Everyone around him starts cheering him on: Come on, Scooter, you can do it. Give 'em hell, Scoot. Slam it, buddy.

You can make eighty-seven bucks and we'll see Susie's tits. Do it for us, man, Jay says.

Susie. Susie. Susie. A couple of guys standing around the table start chanting. Susie laughs and lifts the bottom of her shirt just enough so we can see her cute little bellybutton.

The guys cheer. One asks if he can see them anyway. Susie ignores him.

Come on! Don't be a fucking pussy, screams this large steroid without a neck who everyone calls Moose. Wherever you find a Scooter, there must be a Moose in close proximity. Moose is standing by the counter with two of his friends. All three have arms the size of telephone poles and are spitting Skoal into the same empty coffee can. Moose is holding it, of course. As far as I can tell, Moose is the only one of the three who communicates through speaking. The other two are grunting and crushing beer cans on their foreheads to the squeals and giggles of two sorority girls.

Okay, I'm going to grease the wheel a little bit, Quimby says. He reaches into his wallet and pulls out three one-dollar bills and a ten spot. He dangles them in front of Scooter's face and places them on top of the pile.

One hundred dollars, Quimby says, winking at some girl standing across from him. She smiles.

Everyone cheers. I find myself clapping along with them.

And don't forget! He will also see Susie Perron's beautiful bare breasts. Nipples and everything, Jay says.

Susie giggles and pushes a piece of hair out of her face.

Come on! Quit being a fucking pussy and do the shot, Moose says. His minions grunt and clap their hands together. Loudly. Like they're preparing to run out onto the football field.

Scooter drops his head, pretending to pass out. His jaw hangs open and his mouth makes fishlike movements. The shot sits in front of him.

Don't try the pass out trick, Scooter. We know you're not passed out, Quimby says, shaking him from behind.

Scooter mumbles something and lifts his head.

So what's it going to be? Quimby asks.

Everyone waits, hanging on his answer. Like witnessing this thing will complete an experience. Fill a void. Give the evening some meaning. And maybe it will. How the hell would I know? I never went to college.

Scooter's mouth hangs open. Large beads of sweat drip down his cheeks. Or maybe he's crying. I can't see his eyes because his hat is pulled down too far. Either way, everyone knows he's scared, and I think that's part of what makes this so important. Part of it.

Quimby taps the table with his index finger. So what's it going to be?

Everyone in the kitchen is silent. The music vibrates through the floor from the basement. Scooter lifts the brim of his hat and looks at Susie. She pinches the hem of her shirt with her thumb and index finger and lifts it up a fist's length, revealing the smooth white flesh of her flat belly again.

The same guys cheer. Please, please. For the love of God, let us see those babies, one of them says, panting.

I can almost see Scooter's eyes. But they're half-shut and swollen. I take a sip of my beer.

Scooter looks down at the money. He shakes his head. A couple of people groan. His cheeks are pale.

A hundred beans!

Look at those tits, man! You gotta do it!

Don't be a fucking faggot!

Scooter slowly nods his head.

Cheering. Clapping. Whistling. Quimby walks behind Scooter and starts rubbing his shoulders like he's loosening him up for a fight.

This is it, Scoot. Do it quick and don't worry about puking. It's like taking medicine, my man. Taking your medicine, Quimby says.

I feel a finger dig into my back. I turn around. My roommate Ed is standing there sniffling and smiling. A cute blonde girl is next to him, wringing her hands and looking around the kitchen.

WhatsgoingonSteve?Iheardsomecheering.Istheresomething goingon?Whatsallthenoiseabout?BythewaythisisCindy, Ed says, wiping his nose with his sleeve.

Where'd you get the coke? I ask.

OhCindyknowssomeguywhosoldusagram.Goddamnfuck-ingdrips.Idofferyousomebutyouknow?Whatsgoingonhere?

Yeah, what's going on? Cindy asks. She's *really* cute.

This guy is about to drink his own puke for a hundred bucks, I say.

Oh, Jesus! That's Scooter, Cindy says.

Uh-huh.

Ahundredbucks?Nofuckingway!Nofuckingway!Thats sickshitman.Sickshit, Ed says, sniffling and wiping and sniffling.

Scooter looks around. Some of the girls are cringing or turning their heads or covering their faces with their hands. Scooter looks down at the shot glass. He visibly swallows a lump in his throat. He looks helpless. Lost. Scared. His hand reaches for the shot glass.

Jay gives Scooter two thumbs up.

Moose and his friends start clapping.

Susie cups a tit and squeezes it a little.

Give him some air, Quimby says, parting the crowd with his arms.

Scooter picks up the shot glass. He tilts his head and falls backwards onto the floor, still in his chair. The shot glass breaks. Everyone gasps. Scooter is not moving. I notice a small pool of blood around his head.

Oh my God! He's dead! the girl with the spiked red hair screams, pointing at the blood.

He's not fucking dead! Quimby says. He kneels down beside Scooter, slapping him on the cheek.

Scooter is out for the count, but Quimby is right. His chest is moving.

All right, is anyone sober enough to drive? We need to get him to the emergency room, Quimby says. The pool of blood spreads across the kitchen floor.

I slug back the last sips of my beer, push by Ed and Cindy and leave the kitchen. Everyone is panicking. Or maybe it's something else—not panic, but something else. I think about looking for Michelle, but decide to leave instead.

I walk outside. It's a cool night in late October. I'm standing in the porch light. I take a deep breath and feel the cold air in my lungs. I see it in front of my face when I exhale. It's not unusual to get snow this early in the White Mountains.

But I'm not ready for it. I don't know if anybody is.

THE
ANSWERING
MACHINE

I.

BEEP.

Hey, Julie, baby. It's me. Mark. I just wanted to call and tell you that last night was a good time. Call me later.

Beep.

I saved the message and played it again. Just to confirm that I heard it right.

Beep.

Hey, Julie, baby. It's me. Mark—I stopped the machine.

I turned to her, stunned and disappointed. She told me it was over between them.

We'd just returned from a movie—some Adam Sandler film where he played a moron that triumphed in a witless world. Funny. So funny my diaphragm hurt from laughing. Julie said I needed to laugh more. I was too serious and needed to loosen up. I laughed at the movie. Hard. Very hard. And there we were standing in the living room, listening to Mark Frazier on our answering machine, thanking Julie for "a good time" the previous evening. Definitely not funny.

What? What is he talking about? I thought it was over with him, I said, trying to stay calm.

She fidgeted with her hands, not saying anything. Just staring down at her feet. Or maybe it was the rug. Maybe it was both. She twirled a strand of her long brown hair around her index finger then unfurled it. Twirled, unfurled. Twirled. She lit a cigarette and told me that Mark was probably coked up and saying those things to fuck with me, that he's just jealous because she's with me and not him. Then she laughed. One of those forced laughs where the person is trying to lighten the mood—ha, ha, ha. Cough. Nothing.

Why are you still hanging around him? I asked. I don't want you hanging around his apartment or his band rehearsals. Are you still...?

She tilted her head slightly toward her shoulder and looked at me with big eyes. God, I loved it when she looked at me like that. But I wouldn't let it work. I was serious.

I'm serious, I said. I'm half-tempted to call the cops and tell them about the little coke ring he's running out of his apartment.

She turned pale and ran over to me. She grabbed my hand. I tried to look away. Remain strong and stolid. But I couldn't. I looked into those big eyes and broke. Too much of that look did that to me. She kissed my cheek. The smoke from her cigarette was in my face. She told me he was harmless.

Harmless? I asked.

She said he was harmless.

Is there anything going on between the two of you? I asked. I just don't understand why he would call the apartment.

She said there was nothing going on. And that I had to laugh more. Like Adam Sandler. She considered Adam Sandler a man who knew how to laugh. I read too many serious books. I should watch more movies, like *Happy Gilmore*.

She kissed me lightly on the lips. I could taste the cigarette. I had quit for over two years, but I considered asking her for a drag.

Instead I kissed her back.

II.

Beep.

Kevin. I bet she's sleeping right now. She must be because she was at my place all night. I came in her mouth and everything. You really should watch her. I'm wondering if she'll come by tonight for another round, if you know what I mean. You don't mind. Do you, Kevin? Buddy?...Watch her.

Beep.

I walked down the hallway and glanced into the bedroom. Julie was asleep, a small lump under a crumpled sheet. I could hear her soft snores. The afternoon sun cascaded through the cracks in the closed blinds. A small sleeping lump and soft snores and tangled brown hair on a pillow. Julie. Holding a purple stuffed frog she'd had since she was a little girl. She kept it on the bed. She told me when we moved in that it was a purple frog because purple frogs are unique and her daddy always said she was unique. His sweet little purple frog. Julie. She lived with me for two years and sometimes we thought about marriage, talked about it on Sunday nights with our heads turned on the pillows, facing each other. We talked about it before *he* showed up. Before *he* found his way into her life. Before *he* put that shit in front of her. No. Julie wasn't a fucking junkie whore. She was a small sleeping lump under crumpled sheets. She snored softly. She was a purple frog.

I sat down on the edge of the bed. I ran my hand through her hair. It was damp. She stirred, rubbing her eyes and looking up at me. She smiled and called me baby. I kept running my hand through her hair.

Julie, we have another message on the machine, I said.

She didn't say anything at first. Then she asked who called. I told her it was Mark Frazier. She wanted to know why he called. And I told her that too. She said she was home all last night. I did remember her coming to bed with me. But why was she still sleeping in the afternoon? Why didn't she go out and look for a job like she said she was going to do? Why was she always so tired? She said she felt a little depressed and couldn't get out of bed. I asked her if she was still seeing Mark Frazier. She didn't say anything. I asked her if she was fucking Mark Frazier. She said she wasn't fucking Mark Frazier. I had to believe her. She wasn't fucking Mark Frazier. I still wasn't sure if she was fucking Mark Frazier or not. I stopped running my hand through her hair and turned my back to her. I wanted a cigarette. Two and half years. Fuck it.

Julie sat up in bed. She was wearing one of my T-shirts and nothing else. She kissed the back of my neck and told me that nothing was going on between her and Mark Frazier. She asked me to lay in bed with her. I kicked off my shoes and took off my tie. I lay down beside her. She kissed my forehead. My nose. My mouth. She took off the T-shirt. She was naked. She unbuttoned my shirt. Pressed her warm cheek against my chest. She licked my nipple. My stomach. Reached for my belt buckle. I closed my eyes. For a second, I thought of her doing that to Mark Frazier. But then I cleared my head of everything. Other than her mouth. Warm. Wet. Soft.

III.

blink. blink. blink. blink. blink. blink.

I came home. It was late. I'd been drinking. But not drunk. Julie wasn't home. Where was she? I looked at the machine.

blink. blink. blink. blink. blink. blink.

I could hear his voice. Bastard. Yeah. *Julie's here. Sucking my cock.* I stood with my finger over the button. blink. blink. His voice. *Watch her, Kevin. Watch her.* Where was she? She said she'd be home. Clock said 1:32. I pressed the button.

Beep.

Kevin, it's me. Listen, Kevin, she said and exhaled. *It's over. I can't. I just. I just can't. It's over. Goodbye.*

Beep.

My knees were weak. I fell onto the couch. My stomach hurt. Over? Over. Over, over, over, over, over. Done. It was October. Julie was gone. Two years. Purple frog. Gone. I stood up. I wanted a cigarette. I put on my jacket. Took off my jacket. Didn't need it. Julie was gone. I went to find her. I walked down Perley Street. Our street. Turned left on South State Street. Walked for a while. I looked for lighted windows. Places where Julie might be. Nothing was lighted. It was late. It was Friday. Why weren't the windows lighted? It may have been later than I thought. The last time I looked it was 1:32. It may have been later. Julie was gone. It's over. She said it in her message. Done. There were no lighted windows. I turned left on Pleasant Street. Buildings. Houses. No lighted windows. I turned left on South Street. Passed the Courthouse. No Julie. I walked and walked and walked and walked. It was late. I turned on Thorndike Street. On my right in a yellow house. A light in the attic. I looked at the light. I hated the light. I wished the light was Julie. I hoped the light wasn't Julie. I wished she was there. I hoped that she wasn't there. I wished she'd come back home. I came to the porch. I knocked on the door. It was late. My knuckles were warm. But my body was cold. No answer. I knocked again. Louder. The porch light flicked on. I took deep breaths. It had to be Julie. It couldn't be Julie. It had to be Julie. The door crept open.

An eye peered out from the crack. What the fuck do you want, the eye said. Is Julie there, I said. There's no Julie here. Now get the fuck out of here. It's 2:30 in the fucking morning. The door slammed. The light was still on in the attic. I looked at the light. I wanted a cigarette. I knocked again. Louder. The door flew open. A middle-aged man. Bearded. Pot-bellied. In his underwear. Had a shotgun in his hand. Snapped off the safety. Listen you sick fuck, he said. You have ten seconds to get the fuck off my property or I'm going to shoot first and ask later. I put my hands in the air. I'm sorry, I said. I have the wrong house. I stumbled over the steps. Walking backwards. I turned and ran. I ran and ran and ran and ran and ran. Full sprint. Julie? Purple frog? I stopped. Tried to catch my breath. Julie was fucking Mark Frazier. Julie was gone. It was over. I stared down at the ground. Under a streetlight I saw a half-smoked cigarette. I picked it up. Put it between my lips. I needed a lighter. Julie was gone.

SOUTH

OF

CONCORD

As Cindy ran her fingers slowly through Steve's long hair, Ed noticed she'd been growing her nails. She was also painting them. Red. Sexy, he thought. Very sexy. For the two months Cindy and Ed were together, she had always kept her nails closely clipped and neatly filed. The closest she'd come to polish was a thin layer of strengthener she brushed over the cuticles to keep them from growing over the nail.

"I'm telling you, man, you wouldn't believe the mustache on this girl. It's insane. Out of control. Completely. Out of control. Right?" Steve said, slapping his hand down on Cindy's thigh. He noticed Ed, sitting on a beat-up recliner by the window, watching them with a doleful look spread across his thin, unshaven face. He took his hand off Cindy's leg.

"I don't want to be mean about it, but she really should consider waxing. It's almost as thick as Steve's when he grows it," Cindy said. "In fact, she looks a little bit like you, sweetie."

"Fuck off," Steve said, nudging an elbow softly into her ribs.

Ed smiled humorlessly and looked away. The living room seemed exceedingly bright in the mid-morning. He stared at the plaster chipping off the walls and ceiling. The television droned in the corner. *The Jerry Springer Show.* A guest who'd been sleeping with his cousin was about to confess that he'd also been screwing her sister. The man reminded Ed of his Uncle Al—bearded and pot-bellied with his hair combed over a bald spot. Ed turned away from the television and gazed out the second floor window at a gray bird standing on a telephone wire. He was reasonably sure that, unlike himself, the bird had been far away from Plymouth and the White Mountain Region. In fact, the bird had probably been south of Concord. Ed had been to Concord a number of times visiting friends, but that was the extent of his travels.

"Anyway, if you get the chance, you really should go to the college library and see this chick. The mustache is unbelievable," Steve said.

Ed drifted off. He and Steve had moved to Plymouth two years before from Campton, where they grew up and their parents still lived. Steve followed the Grateful Dead for three years after high school, and Ed stayed at home and worked for his father making maple syrup on their small plot of land. When Steve returned, he and Ed moved into a trailer in Campton and worked at various restaurants around the ski resorts in Waterville and Lincoln—first as dishwashers and eventually making their way up to short-order cooks. They finally decided to move to Plymouth to be closer to the college, the weekend parties and drunken coeds—an atmosphere more accommodating to single men in their mid-twenties.

In Plymouth, they lived the college experience without the stress of final exams or term papers. Occasionally they sold LSD to the students to help pay the rent on the blighted second floor dump they lived in. At a frat party that fall, Ed met Cindy and they started dating. A month later, Steve took a job as a cook at the Snowy Owl, where Cindy worked. Shortly after that, Cindy and Ed split, and Cindy and Steve began dating. Ed just watched, claiming to be unbothered, but quietly withdrawing.

"Why were you at the library?" Ed asked, watching the gray bird and wondering how it managed to stand on the live wire without being electrocuted.

"I was researching something," Cindy said, shifting on the couch.

"Oh," Ed said. He thought it had something to do with the lightness of the bird, but he'd also seen larger birds on that same telephone wire. He wondered what the bird was still doing in Plymouth in December. Birds usually flew south. But it had been a warm winter.

"Hey, you want to go get a beer later?" Steve asked, trying to flag Ed's attention. "I have the night off."

"I'm not up to it," Ed said. "I really should be looking for a job."

"I can get you a job at the restaurant, man. I told you that. They just hired a new guy and they're still looking for more cooks and dishwashers," Steve said, glancing at Cindy, who shook her head.

"I really don't want to work in restaurants anymore."

"Well, let's go get a beer and a newspaper, and you can look at the help-wanted ads at the bar."

"I really can't." Ed kept watching the bird. He'd seen squirrels on the wire as well. They were far heavier than birds. Far heavier.

"You want to smoke?"

"Okay," Ed said. A little pot would help him focus. Perhaps the bird would fly south of Concord that very day into Boston, maybe New York City. Ed had a picture of the Manhattan skyline on his bedroom wall. Someday, he told himself, he'd go to New York City and ride a subway.

Steve pulled out a bag of weed from his pocket. He reached under the couch for the bong, pinched a bud out of the bag and stuffed it into the bowl. He passed the bong and a lighter to Ed, who grabbed it without turning his head from the window.

The bird flew away. Figures, Ed thought, and lit the bong.

Ed returned from Fox Park, where he'd spent two hours in a small playground set back in the woods. He'd stared blankly at a full moon, sitting on a swing and swaying slowly with his toes dragging through the sand. He avoided walks and the park during the daylight. But there was something about the stillness of the woods at night; something about the playground, where during the afternoon the children from the Daycare Center across the street romped on the swings, the jungle gym and teeter-totters. He'd sat in the chilled winter night, rocking back and forth on that swing, thinking of New York City and skyscrapers.

As he walked into the dark apartment, he turned on the lights and made his way to his bedroom. He noticed the door to Steve's room shut as he passed it in the hallway. He went into his bedroom, separated from Steve's by a thin wall, and sat down on his bed, which was nothing more than a box spring with an old mattress on top of it. He put a pillow under his head and stared at the ceiling. When he was a teenager, he'd had a poster of Cindy Crawford covering her bare chest with crossed arms pinned to the ceiling of his bedroom. He remembered staring at the poster while he lay in bed masturbating. Glancing up at the white ceiling—cracked and chipping like the walls—he realized that there was nothing for him to look at anymore except the poster of the Manhattan skyline. There was a closet, a dresser, the box spring and nothing. He shut off the light, turned his head on the pillow and attempted to sleep. Then the noises started.

Her moans tickled his eardrums—made them itch. He squeezed his eyes shut and pulled the pillow over his head in an attempt to suffocate the sound, trying to erase the image of Cindy's back arched and her slim silhouette on the bedroom wall. He saw himself, again beneath her, his hands relaxed on her hips as she rocked tranquilly back and forth. Then he saw himself washed away in the undertow and replaced by Steve, as Ed floated alone in nothing. The noises became louder, the moans sharper. Turning over on his stomach, he buried his face deep into the pillow.

When the noises finally stopped, he stared up at the cracked plaster in the moonlight. He thought about birds, telephone wires and women with mustaches.

Ed cracked an egg on the side of the pan and watched as the white around the yolk fried, gently sizzling in the vegetable oil. He poked at the yolk with the spatula.

The apartment was quiet, with the exception of a stirring from Steve's room. He looked out the kitchen window and noticed that Steve's car was gone. He must be working lunch, Ed thought, and glanced at the clock in the living room. It was already close to noon.

Ed had spent the morning lying in bed, suffering through a

panic attack. These attacks had begun surfacing, inexplicably, shortly after he'd broken up with Cindy and quit his job at the William Tell Restaurant. During an attack, he confronted his own mortality. His heart raced frenetically, seemingly on the verge of cardiac arrest; he became dizzy and disoriented; his arms tingled as he struggled to breathe, gasping for air at irregular intervals. He lay in bed clutching his pillow, unsure of whether his heart would explode or his lungs collapse from lack of oxygen. Sometimes the attacks could last upward of two hours. He'd meant to go to a doctor for medication, but he didn't have insurance and would have rather dropped dead of cardiac arrest than have to pay the medical bill. When the attacks passed, he'd gather himself, exasperated, and move through his day as the threat of another one lurked.

As the egg cooked, Ed glanced at the telephone lines. No birds. The toilet flushed in the bathroom.

Cindy walked into the kitchen smoking a cigarette, wearing one of Steve's T-shirts and a pair of tight gray exercise shorts. Her blond hair was pulled back into a ponytail, exposing the flesh of her neck.

"Hi," Cindy said, pulling a chair out from the kitchen table.

"I didn't know you were still here," Ed said, scooping up the egg and dropping it onto a plate.

"Yeah, I'm still here. Is that a problem? I can leave—"

"No. It's not a problem. Do you want an egg?"

"No. But I'll have some coffee, if you have any made."

Ed was thankful that she didn't want an egg. Breaking eggs depressed him. He grabbed a coffee mug from the cupboard and filled it with the rest of the coffee he'd brewed half an hour earlier. He placed the cup and a carton of old milk in front of Cindy on the kitchen table.

"Thanks," she said, smelling the milk, then pouring some into the coffee.

"You're welcome."

He sat down across from her. He looked at his plate and tried to forget the sounds he'd heard the previous night. He remembered the morning after they'd first slept together. They sat in the same chairs, at the same kitchen table, in the same apartment, smiling at each other. It seemed to be a very long time ago. Now they sat across from each other, having become, in less than three months, nothing in each other's lives. There wasn't any intimacy or friendship or even eye contact. There was nothing except the sound of Ed's fork scraping against the plate.

"How've you been? I'm a little worried about you, Ed."

He let his fork drop onto the plate. He looked up at her. "I need you to tell me something," he said.

"What is it?"

"I need you to tell me about that girl. The one in the library."

"What?"

"The girl the two of you were talking about yesterday. The one with the mustache," Ed said, staring at her, expressionless.

"I don't know what to tell you, Ed. She had a mustache. That's about it. That's all there really is to tell."

"That's not good enough. I need you to describe her for me. I want to see her in my head."

"You're acting weird. You need to get a hold of yourself," Cindy said. "I'm going to take a shower." She grabbed her coffee and stood up from the chair. As she turned to leave the kitchen, Ed picked up the half-eaten egg with his hand and threw it at her back. She spun around, startled.

"It doesn't fly. Does it, *Cynthia*?"

"Fuck you, Ed." She turned and walked out of the kitchen, the yolk smeared on the back of Steve's T-shirt.

He sat at the kitchen table looking at the egg on the floor. Dead, dead, dead. Fried. Like it had stepped too hard on a telephone line.

Ed sat at the kitchen table in the late afternoon and circled potential jobs in the *Penny Saver* while pulling crushed cigarette butts from the ashtray and smoking them down to the filter. There were a variety of jobs that he felt qualified for—painting houses, moving furniture, washing dishes, pet sitting. The sweat and grunt work. However, when he picked up the phone to call some of the numbers, he was met with dead silence. The sound of nothing. He checked the phone cord. It was plugged into the wall. He tapped the phone against the edge of the kitchen table, shook it, flicked the receiver with his index finger. Nothing.

He walked into Steve's bedroom, where there was a second phone. The shades were pulled down. He searched for the phone. The last rays of daylight coming through a window at the end of the hallway provided just enough visibility for him to find it. He could smell the raspberry body spray that Cindy used. It clung to the bed sheets, lurked in the air; the room smelled like Cindy. Ed sat on the edge of Steve's bed and checked the phone. Nothing.

"What are you doing?"

Ed looked up. Steve was standing in the doorway.

"I'm checking the phones. The line is dead. Did we pay the phone bill last month?"

Steve squinted and ran his hand along the wall, turning on the light.

"Yeah, we paid the phone bill. Maybe the lines are just down. I'll check with the neighbors. But I need to talk to you first," Steve said, reaching in his jacket pocket and taking out his pack of Marlboros. He placed one between his lips without lighting it.

"About what?" Ed asked.

"Cindy came in to work as I was leaving. She said the two of you had a little talk this morning, and you threw an egg at her. Is that true?"

"It was cooked," Ed said, looking down at the floor where one of Cindy's bras sat on top of a pile of soiled clothes.

"It doesn't fucking matter. I mean, you said you didn't have a problem if I dated her. Now you're acting just fucking weird around us. You rarely talk. I mean, you said it was okay with you. What were we supposed to do?"

"You should've known!" They both looked at each other, like the voice had come from someone outside of the room.

"All I could do was ask you, man. You said it was okay," Steve said, pulling the unlit cigarette from his mouth.

"It's *not* okay, Steve. It will *never* be okay. As long as I have to watch the two of you together, fucking massaging each other's heads, kissing and screwing every night, it will be everything but *okay*. You should've known never to put a girl between friends." Ed stood up and stared at Steve, who kept his head down, looking at the floor.

"You said it was okay."

"The phone's dead," Ed said. He walked briskly past Steve, down the hallway, down a flight of stairs and out the front door of the apartment. He turned left onto High Street and headed down the hill toward Lamson Library.

Ed hadn't been to a library in the seven years since he'd graduated high school. As he walked through the front doors he was lost in the thick silence and forgot his initial intention in coming. As a girl with a backpack strapped to her shoulders nearly ran him over on her way out, he remembered. The mustache.

He roamed the first floor, casting sidelong glances at the desk workers manning the reference stations. He walked through the rows between bookshelves and stared up in amazement at the vastness of the written word, the vastness of human thought. It occurred to him that nearly every idea in those books came from places south of Concord.

He climbed the stairs to the second floor. Students sat at big wooden tables flipping listlessly through heavy volumes. Ed found himself in front of a reference desk. An older, skinny man, who looked like he ran marathons and ate bran cereals peered at him over a computer. A tuft of wild gray hair grew out of each of his ears, and a pair of reading glasses rested on the bridge of his long, thin nose.

"Can I help you with something, young fella?" His voice was high.

Ed froze, looking blankly at the man. "Um, yeah. I need to take out a book on birds."

"Well, that's a pretty broad subject. Is this for a class?" The man sprung out of his chair and onto his feet.

"I'm not a student," Ed said, while the man seemed to jog in place.

"Not a student? Well then, young fella, you need to go to the front desk and get yourself a library card," he said, sitting back down. "You come see me after you get one. We'll get you some books about birds. How's that sound?"

"Good," Ed said, and walked back down the stairs to the front desk.

A slender, middle-aged woman with her hair pulled into a tight bun sat behind the desk, typing on a computer. Her long fingers tapped at the keyboard. Behind her was an office with the door wide open and the lights turned off. Ed coughed into his hand, and the woman looked up.

Her mouth smoothed into a bashful smile, but her eyes seemed scared—wide and glossy. "Can I help you with something?" she asked in a frail voice.

"Yes, I need to get a library card," Ed said.

From the office, a shadowy figure approached the door, popped its head out for a quick glance and disappeared back into the dark.

"You can get one right here," the woman behind the desk said. "It will only take a few minutes." Her hands moved nervously through stacks of paper; she kept tripping over her fingers. She reached under the counter and opened a drawer. "Shoot," she whispered to herself.

"Is everything all right?" Ed asked.

"Oh, yes. Yes. I just can't find the application forms. If you'll just hold on a second?" She smiled, then winced, wringing her hands. "Laura? Could you bring out a stack of card application forms from the office?"

The light flicked on in the office. A few moments later, a young woman came out with a stack of yellow forms in her hand. Ed watched her as she approached the desk.

Her dark brown hair was in a long braid. Her body was skinny and boyish. Two skinny white legs protruded from a loose, knee-length skirt. Her gaunt face and pallid skin made it look as though she'd never left that darkened back office. Her thin lips seemed siphoned of all color. She had a grayish, downcast mouth. Above the barely visible top lip stood a thick growth of brown hair.

Ed stared as she handed the forms to the other woman. Her eyes looked straight down at the floor. Then, like the sunrises he'd witnessed in Fox Park, they lifted and met his for a suspended second. He became drunk in the silence. The patch of hair beneath her nose seemed to disappear. He felt no lust or desire, just an overwhelming sense of release. His jealousy over Steve and Cindy; the feelings of restlessness and insecurity; the sharp sting of failure were washed away by the tranquility in her eyes.

Ed smiled, and she began to smile back, but instead she dropped the application forms on the counter, turned and scurried back to the office. The light flicked off. She returned safely to the same shadow from which she had manifested.

The other woman picked up the stack of application forms and placed them in the desk drawer. She removed the top one and placed it in front of Ed. "There you go," she said.

Ed looked at the woman. "I forgot a pen," he said. He turned from the desk.

"We have plenty of pens here," the woman called to him. Ignoring her, he walked out the front entrance.

He slipped comfortably back into the cold night. He looked up at the sky. The dull moon sat on the horizon between the dark forms of the White Mountains. He thought about the moon over the Manhattan skyline and how even on clear nights, it probably wasn't as bright as it was on this hazy night in New Hampshire.

He stretched his arms over his head. He contemplated walking to Fox Park and sitting on a bench, watching the moon until the early morning, but it was too cold. He decided instead to go back to the apartment.

He could smell in the evening air that it was going to snow. The birds would be flying south of Concord soon, resting on telephone wires along the way.

A
Long,
Warm
Winter

KAREN told me that writer's block didn't exist, that it was just some crap I made up because I wasn't writing. This was coming from a waitress. But she had a point. It wasn't that I *couldn't* write. Some nights I sat in front of the word processor and watched, almost independent of the process, as pages and pages poured out onto the screen. Then, after reading what I'd written, I'd tear it all up. Discouraged and trying to write for a living without a publisher or even an agent, I'd lay down on the rigid mattress and wait for Karen to come home from work while chain-smoking until my lungs hurt. For the past three weeks, however, I hadn't written a word. Once again, it wasn't that I *couldn't* write; I chose not to. As I lay on the bed staring at the ceiling, Karen was in the bathroom getting ready for work.

We lived in a motel room outside Lincoln, New Hampshire, and paid the rent weekly to the aged couple that owned the place. The Petersons had forgotten how to smile after they purchased the Lost River Motel in the mid-Nineties with their life savings—a modest chunk of change they put away for the day the kids left the nest and they could move into the White Mountains from Concord.

For a few lucrative seasons, it flourished; however, three mild winters and poor ski seasons in a row had taken its toll on the tourist industry and the Petersons. Mr. Peterson reminded me each week that if the business didn't pick up they'd have to close and try to sell by the end of February. It was the middle of January, and that was Mr. Peterson's subtle way of telling us we'd be looking for a new place to live shortly. He also took to drinking heavily and was usually half in the bag by dinnertime. We'd watch him from the window in our room as he stumbled through the parking lot with a bottle of Seagram's in his hand, shrugging at the sky and swearing under his breath.

Karen came out of the bathroom dressed in a white polo shirt and beige khakis. Her long blond hair was pulled back into a tight ponytail. The slow ski industry had also affected her. She waited tables at the Snowy Owl, a restaurant near Loon Mountain, and lived primarily on tips. I worked as a busboy at the same restaurant three nights a week while I was supposedly finishing my novel. But, like I said, I had chosen not to write, so I spent the evenings that Karen worked chain-smoking and glancing at the word processor.

Karen picked through the soiled laundry on the floor by the bed looking for her apron. I could tell by her exaggerated sighs that she was upset. She hated waiting tables. She had a degree in Psychology from the University of Colorado, but realized after graduation that it was either social work or graduate school. The idea of more school didn't appeal to her, and waiting tables paid better than social work. Either way she'd be dealing with nuts, she figured.

I crushed out my cigarette in the ashtray on the nightstand, sat up and smiled at her. The room was a simple arrangement—a queen-sized bed, a flimsy refurnished dresser with a television on top and the remote control screwed to the nightstand, and a small table in front of the window where my word processor sat, the keys collecting dust. The bathroom, at the far end of the room, was the only place we could get away from each other. When we fought, one of us—usually Karen—ran for the bathroom and locked the door behind her, our mutual shouts muted by the thick oak. We kept the blinds drawn over the window, giving the room a cavernous effect in the late afternoon. I watched Karen bent over and cursing because she still couldn't find her apron. I coughed conspicuously.

"Not now, Bill. I'm already late for work," she said.

"Oh, come on, sweetie. Be a sport," I said, lighting another cigarette.

"I CAN'T FIND MY FUCKING APRON!" She began throwing handfuls of clothes around the room.

The place was too small to really lose anything. I reached over, ran my hands under the bed and pulled out her apron, smiling like some amateur magician lifting a rabbit from his hat. She looked at it dangling from my fingertips and snatched it.

"Now, now. Don't we have a temper tonight?" I said. The daylight was passing away as the sun slipped behind the mountains. I looked at the alarm clock on the nightstand. It was 4:10. The short days drained me.

"How much longer do we have to do this?" Karen said, pulling a cigarette from my pack and sitting down beside me on the bed.

"Until we save enough money to move back out west," I said. I knew this wasn't the answer that she wanted to hear. She wanted to hear something new. She wanted to hear an answer where I would save us, provide for us and become a responsible man, a pillar of strength. She didn't want the down-on-his-luck wannabe writer who won one lousy short story contest in college and had been collecting stacks of rejection slips since. I rubbed her knee softly. All the sexual energy drained from my body like air squeezed from a balloon. I looked down at the rug.

Karen placed her small hand over mine. It just barely covered my knuckles. Her fingers stroked my own. That was all we had, and I knew I'd spend the next six months looking for something else—something as tangible as a manuscript, a decent paycheck or a warm winter coat without holes in the sleeves. I'd have to try to write us out of that small, moldy motel room in the middle of nowhere and into the places I'd promised Karen when we met in Boulder eight months before. I'd try to become the confident young man who had convinced her to move back east with him as he finished what would be the next Great American Novel. I'd try, but like the stories I wrote and tore up afterwards, it seemed to be nothing but an exercise in futility. Karen was a good woman, the kind my college buddies used to call "a keeper." I felt an uncomfortable churning in my stomach as she clung to my hand. That feeling deep inside my chest told me it wasn't going to last much longer.

Karen must've sensed this and rather than ask more questions, she wrapped her arms around my back and rested her head on my lap. "It's all right. We'll be all right," she said.

I knew she didn't believe it. Any of it.

"I know." I lied. "You're going to be late for work."

She sat up with her cigarette between her fingers and gave me a quick kiss on the lips as she grabbed her purse from the nightstand. She walked slowly out the door, looking over her shoulder at me sitting on the edge of the mattress. I tried to reassure her with a smile, but my eyes wouldn't cooperate.

"Write something wonderful," she said, shutting the door behind her. I knew I wouldn't turn on that word processor for the next six hours.

I sat on the bed for an hour staring at a painting above the television set. I couldn't understand how I'd overlooked it as nothing more than a wall ornament for the two months we'd been living in the motel. It was a print in a tawdry wooden frame of an impoverished 19th century Parisian street corner during a cold winter; the plaintive villagers, bundled up in shawls and scarves, stood in front of a decrepit vegetable cart with an old wooden wheel half-buried in the snow on the sidewalk. The villagers' eyes were downcast, not daring to look up at the frozen world around them. I found myself looking for the smallest morsel of food lying in the snow by their feet—a gaunt carrot or a bruised tomato. I tried not to think of anything else—Karen, the typewriter, the west, my promises. I began to wonder what had possessed the Petersons to hang such a sullen picture in a room they were trying to rent to strangers on vacation. It seemed unfathomable. I needed to talk to Mr. Peterson.

I found him in the small room behind the front desk in the lobby. As I walked in, he poured the remains of a fifth of Seagram's Seven into a tall glass with ice. He topped it off with a splash of flat-looking ginger ale and mixed it with his index finger. He was watching the six o'clock news with a dull gaze, waiting for the weather report. He was wearing the same clothes I'd seen him in since we'd checked in—stained undershirt and a pair of navy blue Dickies. An immense heft of flab hung over his waistline like a blubbery landslide of flesh. He turned his head and looked indifferently over his shoulder at me. Unshaven and red-eyed, he brusquely asked, "What the hell you want?"

"Um, I wanted to talk to you about that painting, the one hanging in our room. How did it get there?" I phrased my question carefully, trying to find the right words to use with an alcoholic losing everything to another mild winter.

"What the hell are you talkin' about, boy," he said, taking a long slug from the glass.

"There's a picture in our room—a painting hanging over the television. It's possibly the most depressing thing I've ever seen. Why did you hang it up in a room you're supposedly trying to rent to people? Do you think they'll look at the painting, see all these people moping, dying, freezing, starving in the snow and decide to unstrap the skis from the roof of their S.U.V. and stay for another night?" I threw up my hands and watched Peterson for a response.

"Listen, son." He pointed a fat index finger at my chest. "When you got problems like I got, you don't have time to worry about what fuckin' painting is hangin' on the wall of a room you can't afford to heat anyhows. Is it depressin' ya? Is it hurtin' your little feelings? Okay...but let me tell ya somethin', it's a hell of a lot easier to look at some stupid painting than it is at the real thing. At least they got some fuckin' snow. Now if you have a problem with the plumbin', the shitta, the heat, you let me know. But don't come buggin' in the middle of the news about some stupid painting. All right? Now shut your hole, the weather's on." He took another hard pull off his drink and held his breath as a nerdy meteorologist traced a storm front right up the Great Lakes and into Canada with the swoop of his arm.

I turned out of the office and began back to the motel room. As I was walking out, I heard a glass smash against a wall.

I sat back down on the bed with my back turned to the painting. In the corner of my eye the word processor rested idly on the table.

I hadn't punched a key in almost three weeks and didn't have the heart to tell Karen I had abandoned my novel over a month ago. Every night I added some blank sheets of paper to the bottom of the pile to create the illusion of progress. When Karen asked how the novel was going, I pointed to the pile and said, "Slowly, but look. It's getting there."

I walked over to the table, grabbed a handful of blank paper and placed it on the bottom of the pile. I rubbed my hands together. Work completed for the night. I reached over for my pack of cigarettes. Empty.

In the woods of the White Mountains convenience stores can be anything but convenient. The closest one to our motel room was a ten-minute drive on the Interstate or a twenty-minute more scenic back route into town. Karen took her car (which was the more reliable of our two) to work, leaving me with my old Nissan Sentra, which failed to pass inspection the last time around. We only used it for emergencies. I considered being stranded in a motel room with the word processor and the painting for four more hours without cigarettes an emergency.

One of the headlights had been out for close to two months. I'd meant to replace it, but after the car failed inspection, I couldn't see the point. I decided there would be less chance of being pulled over in an illegal vehicle on the back route down the narrow, two-lane Lost River Road. I started the car and waited for the heat to kick in. A still winter chill loomed in the air. I threw the car in reverse and turned left out of the empty parking lot.

Lost River Road wound through the mountains; white birch trees lined one side of the road. The other side followed the Pemigewasset River south into Plymouth. The darkness and winding curves made it dangerous at night, but I took it slow. I needed the drive. The painting and word processor waiting in the motel room kept me steady at thirty miles per hour.

I guided the car around Tuckerman's Curve, which was notorious for its off-road accidents. In the gleam of my one headlight I saw a large, black mass blocking the two-lane road. "What the hell?" I said to myself. I turned down the radio and stepped gently on the brakes, pulling the car over to the side of the road. I kept the headlight on the black heap. I got out and began walking toward it. The wheezes of a dying moose lying on its side with its legs snapped clean in half cut through the cold air. Next to the moose's mammoth frame were the crushed remnants of the automobile that had struck it.

The front end of the car had been squashed like an aluminum can in a metal compressor. The windshield had shattered into thousands of tiny particles of glass—slivers of which were stuck in the moose's side. I knew what remained in the car and took a deep breath before looking inside. The steering wheel, which had been pushed forward under the impact of the collision, had completely scalped the driver. With his head back, his mouth still open, gaping in an eternal scream, and front teeth shattered into jagged stumps, the driver sat dead with his skull cap exposed under trestles of blond blood-stained hair. I stood frozen for about ten seconds before I turned my back to the wreck and vomited on the side of the road.

I felt my legs give out on me. I lay with my head turned away from the accident and my cheek pressed against the cold pavement. The moose continued to wheeze, barely clinging to life. I'd heard when the police showed up at the site of a moose accident and the animal was still alive, an officer put a slug through its head and ended the suffering. But how would the police be notified of the accident? I realized it was my responsibility to get back in the car, turn around and find the nearest telephone to report it. But I couldn't move. I couldn't even turn my head to look again at the accident, much less the driver. I laid very still on the pavement, thinking if I hadn't stopped to visit Peterson; if I hadn't sat on the bed staring at the damn painting; if I hadn't lingered in the motel room that extra ten minutes smelling the dust on the keys of the word processor, it could've been me. This realization pressed heavily on my mind as I assessed every minute detail that had kept me alive—on the pavement near a puddle of my own vomit, but alive.

I finally peeled myself up from the ground and sat with my

knees drawn up and my head between my legs. I sat like that for close to an hour, shivering as every gust of wind cut through the holes in my coat. I didn't think about much. My mind was moving at such a rapid pace it was impossible to catch a full thought for longer than a few seconds. So I stopped trying. I knew I was weeping, but the tears seemed cold and distant as they froze against my cheeks. I was in this fetal position when a set of headlights shone off the shattered side mirror of the mangled car.

An old man got out of a pickup truck and ran towards us. He had a Boston Red Sox baseball cap pulled far over his eyes and the backwoods hunter's beard. He tapped me on the shoulder and looked over at the accident. I looked up at him, my eyes sore with the frozen tears, and waited to hear the sound of his voice.

"What happened here, son?"

There was a trace of liquor on his breath. I stared blankly at him and shrugged my shoulders.

"Are you hurt? You're damn lucky that moose didn't kill you," he said. Then he turned around and caught a glimpse of the driver and the tangled heap of fur and flesh in front of him. "Mary, mother of God," he said under his breath and ran to his truck. I heard him click on a CB radio and start scanning through the channels for help.

The old man came back, put a worn red and black flannel blanket over my shoulders and helped me to my feet. "Come on, son. Let's go wait in the truck where it's warm. The police will be here any minute." He walked me to the truck with his arm around my back. We got inside. He offered me a cigarette. I giggled humorlessly at the irony and placed it between my lips. He struck a wooden match and carried the flame behind his cupped hand towards me, then lit his own. We sat there smoking, saying nothing. I heard the faint sound of sirens approaching, echoing softly through the mountains.

By the time I had calmed down enough to write my statement, it was close to three in the morning. A police officer drove me home from the station in my car, while another one followed us in a cruiser. He pulled into the parking lot and snapped off the one headlight. "You really should get that fixed," he said.

I nodded.

"Are you going to be all right?" the officer said. He was middle-aged and slightly rounded in the belly from many inactive years as a small town cop.

"Yeah," I said, "thanks for the ride." I shook his hand and began walking towards the motel room.

"If we need anything else from you, we'll call. Why don't you try and get some sleep." The officer saluted me with two fingers to the forehead and ducked into the cruiser that had followed us. They slowly pulled out of the parking lot. I watched the tail lights vanish into the distant darkness.

I turned the doorknob of our motel room and crept inside. Karen was still awake and watching an infomercial on television. The police had called her earlier to let her know what had happened. I sat on the edge of the bed and took off my shoes as Karen wrapped her arms around my shoulders.

"Do you want to talk about it?" she said.

"Let's just go to sleep, Karen. We'll talk in the morning," I said, lying back in the bed, still fully clothed.

Karen clicked off the television. Through the small chinks in the blinds, slightly illuminated by the parking lot lights that Peterson had forgotten to turn off before passing out, I saw a few snowflakes begin to fall. I put my arms around Karen. I could still smell a trace of vomit on my T-shirt. I pulled it off and dropped into the pile of soiled laundry. I placed my head between Karen's breasts as she kneaded my hair with her fingernails. I rested my ear against her ribcage, closed my eyes and listened to her heart beat. I opened my eyes to look at the silhouette of the word processor on the wall below the painting. I knew it wasn't going to last much longer.

HUSH

MICHELLE checked her figure in the reflection of a spoon. She cupped her breasts in the palms of her hands and gave them a quick lift while the cooks weren't looking. She pursed her lips, pulled her long blond hair back into a ponytail and resumed drying the silverware with a kitchen rag. Outside the window by the dish station where she was standing, the sun began to set behind Loon Mountain, poking a few weak rays through a mass of gray clouds low on the horizon. The air was brisk and still; it hinted the winter's first storm. In mid-January, the unusually clement weather had taken its toll on the local industries. The motels, restaurants, ski and sport shops, the slopes— all the owners and employees waited for a good blast to bring the tourists up to the White Mountains so the money could start coming in. They could at least salvage the second half of the season.

Allison walked in the back door and through the kitchen. She grabbed her time card and punched in.

Pop. Click.

She approached Michelle from behind and pinched her hip. Michelle jumped forward, nearly dropping the silverware in her hand.

"Jesus, you scared me half to death," she said, spinning around and slapping Allison with the rag.

"How's it going?" Allison asked.

The two girls, both blonde, young and attractive, were dressed identically in beige khakis just snug enough around the hips and thighs to jack up a tip and white polo shirts with the Snowy Owl's insignia—the silhouette of an owl perched on a branch—stenciled on the left breast.

"It's going shitty," Michelle said. "I'm here on a Tuesday night, and it's going to be dead. I don't know why I waste my time at this place." She sighed and rolled her eyes.

"*I* don't want to be here *either*," Allison said, grabbing a handful of silverware and a rag. "I was supposed to go see the Overtones at the Bier House tonight, but get this. I tried calling Brenda to cover for me, but the bitch had her mother answer and tell me she wasn't home. I could hear her in the background. What a bitch, huh?"

Michelle nodded her head. "Bitch," she repeated under her breath.

"Anyway," Allison drew closer to Michelle, putting her hand on her shoulder. "Did you hear about Steve and Melanie?"

Michelle's eyes widened. She grabbed Allison's arm. "No! What?"

"Well, I heard from Brent..."

Nick watched as Steve, who was crouched down eye-level with the flatbed grill, reached underneath with a match and lit the pilot.

"Simple as that, man. Just turn it on, let it heat up and you're ready to rock. The burger and chicken patties are in this walk-in," Steve said as he led Nick around the corner, out of the kitchen toward the back entrance. They stood in front of a thick, wooden door with a rusted metal handle and a padlock hanging from the hinge. Steve pulled it open. A cold white cloud rushed out from the walk-in freezer. They went inside.

"The burgers are over here to your left, and the chicken's right above it on the rack. You get all the frozen stuff here—the chicken fingers, buffalo wings, potato skins, you know, anything dropped in the fry-a-lator." Steve pointed to the boxes on the top shelf. "This is also where we get baked when Mike isn't around. You smoke?"

"Sure," Nick said, looking down at a bag of onions in the corner.

Steve looked at his watch. "Mike won't be in for another hour or so. I got a bowl if you're interested," Steve said. He tightened the red bandana that kept his long blond hair out of his face and tied the rest back with an elastic band.

"Yeah. I'll smoke a little," Nick said. Like Steve, Nick had a grungy appearance—long brown sideburns, an unshaven face and a baseball hat pulled down over his eyes.

"This is some pretty kind shit, man," Steve said, reaching into the pocket of his checkered chef's pants and grabbing a small glass-blown bowl and red Bic lighter.

"Cool. Nice bowl, " Nick said.

Steve smiled. "Thanks, I got it at a Dead show in Eugene in '94," he said and closed the freezer door, leaving it slightly propped open with a torn piece of cardboard from the top of a box of lettuce. He passed the bowl and the lighter to Nick. "You go ahead," he said.

"Thanks, man."

Michelle and Allison stood at the bar, waiting for the restaurant to open. Brent, the bartender, stocked the coolers. Karen came up behind Michelle and Allison and stuck an index finger in each of their lower backs. The girls turned around and acknowledged Karen, then turned back to their conversation.

"So she left with him?" Michelle asked.

Allison nodded. "That's what I heard. Brent was working the bar last night. He saw it."

"Saw what?" Karen asked.

"You promise not to say anything?" Michelle said, raising her eyebrows.

"I promise. What happened?" Karen asked, leaning over further and staring at Michelle.

"Well, rumor has it that Steve left with Melanie last night. Apparently, they were getting pretty close at the bar after work," Michelle whispered. Allison confirmed by nodding her head.

"No *way!*" Karen said, covering her mouth with her hand. "What about Cindy? Does she know?"

"I don't think so. All I know is that Cindy is coming in at 5:30, and Melanie at 6:00. And," Allison said, pausing and looking at Brent, "Steve is working with that new guy tonight."

"Oh-my-God! This could get ugly," Karen said. The three girls looked at each other and nodded.

"All I know is I'm not going to say *anything*," Allison said.

"Me neither," Michelle said.

"Me neither," Karen said.

Brent shook his head.

       "That's about it, man. You'll have the hang of it by the end of the night. If you have any questions, just ask me. And I'll warn you right now, Mike loses his head when it gets really busy. You've worked in restaurants. You know how chefs are."

Nick nodded while tying a white apron around his waist. The weed really slugged him. He had difficulty concentrating; his mind jumped from one thought to the next without fully recognizing any of them. His heart pounded like a snare drum against his ribs. He picked up a garnishing carrot from a metal container and immediately placed it back down.

A teenage kid walked into the kitchen, grabbed a time card and stuck it in the time clock.

Pop. Click.

"What's up, Joe?" Steve said to the kid, who immediately grabbed an apron and put it on over his head.

"What's up, Steve?"

"Hey, come here. I want you to meet the new cook."

Joe, a skinny kid with greasy black hair and scattered acne on his forehead and chin, walked behind the line and stood with his hands in the pockets of his jeans.

"Joe, this is Nick. Nick, Joe," Steve said. "He's the dishwasher."

Nick wiped his hand on his apron and extended it to Joe. Joe shook his hand without making eye contact.

"Good to meet you, Joe," Nick said, smiling weakly as the kitchen spun and his heart raced like a John Bonham drum solo.

"Nice to meet you," Joe said, then hurried into the dish area and started to fill the Hobart machine while removing the previous night's leftover dishes from a black bus bucket.

"He doesn't say much, but he's a hard worker," Steve said. "He just moved up here from Laconia. He dropped out of high school and moved in with his sister, Cindy. That's the girl I've been dating. She'll be here in a little bit. She's a bartender and the floor manager on Tuesday nights." Steve looked at his watch. "Hey, you want to go smoke a cigarette? Everything's all set, and it looks like Mike's going to be late again, so we have to wait on the specials."

Steve reached in his pocket for his pack of Marlboros and stuck one between his lips.

"Yeah, that sounds like a good idea," Nick said.

Cindy walked into the kitchen ten minutes late and punched her time card.

Pop. Click.

She gave a quick wave to Steve and made her way to the waitresses' station where the three girls were huddled in a circle, sipping sodas through straws and waiting for the first party of the night. Cindy's wavy blond hair was clipped back. Her long, black skirt and red silk blouse identified her as the *manager*—not a shift waitress. Standing next to the girls, it was nearly impossible to discern any difference in age. She had turned 30 that October, which had kept her inside her apartment for two days straight. She was petite with slender limbs and small features. Only after looking closely at her face and noticing the tiny wrinkles settled around her eyes was it apparent that she was older. She had been dating Steve, four years her junior, for three months and had consciously traded a serious commitment for an occasional orgasm and a warm body to sleep next to. She had collected a closet full of bridesmaid's dresses while watching each one of her friends slowly, like stubborn bowling pins, get knocked out of the dating pool and thrust into worlds of dinner parties and Little League games in the spring.

"Sorry I'm late. Is everything ready to open? I'll do the seating charts now," Cindy said, removing her coat and slinging it over her arm.

Karen, Allison and Michelle looked at each other, biting down on their bottom lips.

"What is it?" Cindy asked.

Michelle wrung her hands and shook her head. "Cindy, did you hear about Steve and Melanie?"

"I always knew she was a slut," Allison murmured under her breath.

"What are you talking about?" Cindy said, placing her hands on her hips and staring at the three waitresses.

"Well, I heard from Brent," Allison began.

The first order of the night came in. Nick stood blankly with the slip in his hand and waited for Steve to return from Mike's office where he'd taken a phone call.

Steve came back shaking his head. "Mike's not coming in tonight. That was his wife. Looks like I'm in charge," Steve said, grabbing the slip from Nick.

"Oh yeah? What's wrong?" Nick had finally come down to the point where he had a cool, manageable buzz.

"His wife says he's been sick all day, which means he's hungover. The owners have been looking to replace him. He's already gotten three DWIs and a drunken disorderly in Campton, where he lives. Nice guy, but he's gotten himself a bad reputation around the area," Steve said, glancing at the slip and tossing a filet of haddock onto the grill.

"That sucks," Nick said as his eyes followed a dark-haired girl walking in through the kitchen. She grabbed her time card and punched in.

Pop. Click.

"Hey, Melanie," Steve said.

"Hi Steve," Melanie said, turning around and waving with her fingers.

Steve leaned in closer to Nick and shook his head, making clicking noises with his tongue while Melanie made her way to the waitresses' station. "Man, I would love to get me some of that. I swear, if I wasn't with Cindy..." Steve put his hands out in front of him like he was holding female hips and thrust forward with his pelvis.

"Yeah, it's been awhile," Nick said. He watched her walk through the kitchen, hypnotized by her feminine sway. It marked the onset of what the cooks at his last job had called "kitchen porn," a game where the cooks contrived deviant sexual fantasies about attractive waitresses to pass the long, often tedious hours behind the line. Nick would watch pretty young females walk into the kitchen in erratic intervals, picking up hot dinner plates and lifting trays over their heads, then disappearing back into the dining room. He filed these fantasies—mental pictures of their asses, chests and legs—to call upon in his bedroom later that night as he stared up at the ceiling. He conjured up an image of Melanie lying supine and naked, licking her lips with a pink, smooth tongue.

Steve nudged him with his elbow, snapping him out of his trance.

"She is suh-weet," Steve said shaking his head and grabbing a sauté pan from a rack above them.

"Hi, Mel."

"Hi, Melanie."

Allison and Karen stood at the waitresses' station with bright, forced smiles. Michelle was in the dining room attending to the only party.

"Hey, how's it going? Any tables yet?" Melanie asked, putting down her pocketbook and grabbing her apron.

"A few, but it's a Tuesday night. Can you believe that Cindy scheduled four of us? I mean, it's not like anyone is going to come in tonight. I should be the manager. She has no idea what she's doing," Allison said, rolling her eyes.

"Well, she'll probably send you home early," Melanie said. Although she'd been working there for three months and had seniority over Karen, Melanie was still the "new girl" at the Snowy Owl. A single mother and working two jobs, she had little time for the activities that busied most 23 year olds—dating, bar hopping with friends, dancing at clubs. She supposed that had something to do with the reason she would always be the "the new girl" to the other waitresses, aside from the fact that she lived forty minutes away in Ashland, where the rent was cheap and the locals all bore a strange genetic resemblance to one another. This, Melanie thought, had a lot to do with the reasons she befriended Cindy. For Melanie and Cindy, the restaurant wasn't merely a part-time job while going to college, like it was for the other waitresses; it was money they needed to survive. Since she had Robbie three years before and his father left for Ohio, Melanie consciously kissed her "party years" goodbye. Most nights after her shift and a drink at the bar, she went home to a babysitter and an old couch where she watched David Letterman, muted with closed-captioning on, and listened to the slow breathing of her son in the other room.

"Well, I was the second one here, so I'm going home after Michelle," Allison said folding her arms.

Karen turned her back to Allison, looked at Melanie and rolled her eyes.

There was a small dinner rush at 7:00, and some late stragglers still coming into the restaurant at 8:00. By 8:30, Steve and Nick had crumpled the last slip, plucked the last chicken breast sandwich from the grill, pulled the last plate from the oven and dropped the last basket of fries into the fry-a-lator. Joe kept busy in the dish pit, working his way through the dinner plates and silverware while shoving glass racks through the machine for Brent. As the cacophony of kitchen noise faded, Nick followed Steve out to the dumpster with his pack of cigarettes already in his hand.

Steve turned over an empty milk crate and sat under the outside light by the dumpster. "Weird," he said, shaking his head and lighting his cigarette.

"What?" Nick asked, turning over a milk crate for himself and taking the lighter from Steve. The air was brisk and dry, chilling Nick's lungs as he inhaled.

"Cindy hasn't talked to me all night. It's not like we were busy. I asked her what was bugging her, and she just shrugged and walked away. Chicks, man. Chicks." Steve bit his thumbnail while staring at his feet.

"I know," Nick said.

They smoked in silence, their shadows cast over the cold cement in front of them.

"You don't have a girlfriend, huh?" Steve asked, spitting out a piece of his nail.

"No," Nick said.

Steve looked closer at Nick. "How old are you, if don't mind me asking?"

"Thirty-two," Nick said, removing his baseball hat. His hair, closely buzzed, receded to the top of his forehead.

"She's single, you know."

"What?"

"Melanie," Steve said, staring at the head of his cigarette. "She has a kid, though."

"Yeah, she's real cute." Nick stared up at the dull stars wedged between two dark clouds. He looked at the dumpster beside him— large, green and emitting the rancid stench of old garbage. He counted on his fingers the years it had been since he'd woken up with a woman beside him.

"When you have one, you want to be alone. When you're alone, all you think about is how you're going to find one," Steve said, crushing his cigarette on the rubber sole of his sneaker. He stood up and kicked the milk crate against the dumpster.

"Yeah. There's no winning. Only getting by," Nick said, tossing his own cigarette in an empty coffee can filled with dirt.

"Yeah," Steve said running his hand over his face. "It feels like it's going to snow."

"I hate the fucking snow," Nick said.

"Shit, you're living in the wrong place, man," Steve said, pointing towards the mountain, a dark form on the horizon. "Hey, you want to have a beer after work? We get shift drinks."

"Sure. I'm already thirsty. It's been an interesting first day."

"I keep forgetting that."

"What?"

"That it's your first day."

"Yeah, it seems like I've already been here longer."

Steve laughed dryly. "It's seems like I've been here forever."

"How long have you been here?" Nick asked.

"Forever."

They walked back into the kitchen as the back door slammed and echoed through the cold night.

Cindy watched Melanie wipe down her last table. She had waited the entire night for the right opening, the right time to corner her.

Michelle was the first one cut. Allison followed shortly after her. The restaurant was empty with the exception of an old man with a Boston Red Sox cap pulled far over his eyes and a hunter's beard sitting at the bar quietly numbing himself with scotch and water. Melanie and Karen set the tables for the next day, blew out the candles, wiped down the waitresses' station, and began drying silverware in the dish area while they waited for Cindy to check their side-work and send them home.

"Has Cindy been acting strange tonight, or is it me?" Melanie asked Karen.

Karen's eyes widened. "No. I mean...yeah. A little."

"Hmm." Melanie picked up a stack of silverware and brought it to the waitresses' station.

Cindy watched from the dining room.

"All right, man. That's it. Just shut off the ovens." Steve turned the black dial on the ovens from "350" to "Off". "Turn off the fry-a-lator, the grill. Joe is going to mop, so he'll take care of the lights. And we're out of here. Beer time, brother."

Nick smiled. He watched Melanie at the waitresses' station as she took her hair out of the ponytail. It spilled onto her shoulders. He imagined himself reaching over and pushing the hair aside, lightly kissing her neck.

"I'll meet you at the bar," Steve said. "I have to see what's been up Cindy's ass all night." He threw up his hands and headed toward Cindy as she approached Melanie.

Nick punched out.
Click. Pop.

"You bitch!" Cindy pressed her face, nose to nose, against Melanie's. Her arms hung loosely at her sides. Her chest pressed forward.

"What are you talking about, Cindy?" Melanie felt her legs weaken. Her heart raced. Her voice was thin and desperate.

"What do you think I'm talking about? Don't play dumb. I heard everything! I know! I know about you and Steve."

The color flushed from Melanie's face. Her bottom lip quivered. She struggled to form words.

Steve jumped between the two girls. "Hey, what the hell is going on here?"

Cindy hurled a fist at his chest. "Don't play dumb, you fucking bastard! I heard about the two of you. Last night. Sitting together at the bar. Getting comfortable and leaving together. What did you do? Huh? Did you fuck her, Steve?"

Steve grabbed Cindy by the shoulders and shook her. "What the hell are you talking about? We didn't do *anything*. We had a few drinks then went home. Alone."

"Yeah, then why didn't you call me last night?"

"I fell asleep. Ask Ed. I was home last night. Where the hell did you hear this from anyway? Who's starting these rumors?"

"I just, you know, heard it from...a couple of...oh shit...the girls," Cindy said, slapping her forehead. "Oh, Jesus. What's wrong with me? I know better than this. Oh, God. I'm sorry. I'm sorry, Melanie. I should've known better."

Melanie stood motionless, her jaw agape. Slowly, without looking at Steve or Cindy, she picked up her pocketbook and made her way to the time clock.

Click. Pop.

Steve put his arms around Cindy. She was weeping.

"It's all right, baby. You're just overtired. We'll go home now. We'll go to my place, baby."

The bar was empty. Nick sat at a stool with a cigarette in the ashtray. He traced small circles around the mouth of his Bud Light bottle with his index finger.

Melanie sat down two stools away from Nick. She shot a cross look at Brent, who mixed her a margarita and set it in front of her. The expression on Brent's face, a sheepish smile mixed with feigned apology, reminded her of the look Robbie's father gave her when she asked if he'd ever be back.

Nick watched Melanie, hoping to catch a small sign, a glimmer of interest. In his younger days, he might have tormented himself with the idea of approaching her, trying a line or playing it natural—which inevitably sounded like a line anyway. But now he was 32 years old, and, although never comfortable with loneliness, he had learned to accept it. And like the waitresses at the last six restaurants he'd worked at, Melanie would most likely become "kitchen-porn"—an image on his ceiling before falling asleep. It was easier that way. Fantasies didn't emasculate. No matter how lonely it got some nights, it made things easier.

Melanie turned and looked at Nick.

"Hi," Nick said. He wasn't going to bite.

"Have a good first day?"

"I guess. It could've been worse."

"That's good. At least someone…ah, forget it," Melanie said, sipping her margarita.

Nick turned his body on the stool and faced Melanie. His stomach sank. He tried to think of a line, forgetting everything. "Hey, listen. Can I buy that drink for you?"

"Actually, it's a shift drink. It's on the house," Melanie said. She smiled.

"Well, how about the next one?"

"Maybe. As long as you don't get too close," she said, raising her voice for Brent.

"Don't worry," Nick said. "I won't."

SCRAPS

KEVIN hovered over her. His elbows locked. Her brown eyes swirled with lust and anxiety. He planted hard, rapid pecks on her lips, hoping that somewhere in the succession he'd find restraint. He knew in his head what was right. He also knew he'd already crossed too many lines.

"I want you. I want to do this," she said, reaching around his back and pulling him closer. His body collapsed on top of her. Their bare chests pressed together.

Kevin knew if they weren't naked; if the room had a little more lighting; if her soft breasts weren't pressed against his skin; if her firm, youthful legs hadn't spread and wrapped around his waist, he could've stopped. The knowledge made him feel somewhat better as he pushed his hips forward, sliding inside of her. She moaned softly—more of a gasp—as he entered. He did it. There was no going back.

After a couple of short thrusts, the feeling started to build in him. He panicked. It hadn't even been a minute. He tried distracting himself with thoughts of his mother saying a rosary, the Boston Red Sox batting order, walking barefoot over hot coals. It was no use. He gritted his teeth and exploded inside the condom. His body relaxed as he buried his face in the couch.

She ran her fingers through his hair and kissed his earlobes. "That was the best I've ever had, Mr. Cohen," she whispered.

Then it hit him like a brick to the nose. There was no denying it. She was, for a fact, sixteen years old.

He dropped Gina off two blocks from her parents' house and decided to drive around town, rather than going straight back to his apartment. He had lived and taught high school in Concord, New Hampshire for four years. His life had been quiet, defined by patterns and predictability. It wasn't until that fall when his ex-girlfriend, Julie, left him and moved to Boston with the drummer of an Aerosmith cover band called *Sweet Emotion* that things started to come undone. He took it hard, spending long nights drinking Heinekens alone at his kitchen table and staring at old photographs. Gina showed up in his class at the wrong time. He was still rebounding. She was aggressive—coming after school for "extra help," taunting him with tight shirts and short dresses. When she asked him if she could stop by his place to talk about some problems she was having at home, he reluctantly agreed. When she leaned over his kitchen table earlier that night and gently kissed his mouth, he passionately reciprocated, allowing the months of pent up frustration to pour out, drowning his good sense.

Kevin reached into his glove compartment and pulled out a pack of cigarettes. He placed one between his lips and pushed in the car lighter. He'd bought a pack of Marlboros before he'd picked up Gina, who was waiting for him under a streetlight on Pleasant Street. He'd quit for two and a half years. Now he inhaled deeply, the tobacco burning his throat.

He drove past the coffee shop on Main Street that he and Julie used to go to when they needed to get out of the apartment and didn't have money for beer. He remembered how she used to put ice cubes in her coffee and drink it down to get the caffeine buzz. It was before she started using amphetamines, before she started her clandestine meetings with her musician coke dealer friend.

He parked in a spot on Main Street next to the café. He contemplated getting out for a cup of coffee, but decided to keep driving instead. He drove past the Capitol Building, turning onto Green Street and slowing down to look inside the entrance of the police station. He was barely conscious of the road. The picture of Gina's body spread out on the couch, her smooth skin and nubile curves, remained etched in his mind. The way she shyly removed her bra and the first glimpse of her nakedness stroked by the moonlight aroused him as he drove. He pictured her picking up her clothes, giggling and carrying the bundle into the bathroom to dress after sex. As he passed the State Courthouse, he began to comprehend the severity of what he'd done. Dread and panic. The schoolboard, the police, prison. He slammed on the brakes just before rear-ending a white Mercedes stopped at a traffic light. He looked at the clock on the dashboard. It was 11:32. He had to teach in the morning.

The ticking of the wall clock resonated throughout the silent classroom. Kevin removed his glasses, wiped them on his tie and repeated the question.

"So why do you think George killed Lenny at the end?"

He looked around at the students, a class of General Junior English. Four or five of them had their heads down, cradled in their arms. A few of them flipped through the pages of their battered copies of *Of Mice and Men*, pretending to search for an answer. Kevin watched a note being passed in the back of the room from a notorious drug dealer with long red hair, a "Kill 'Em All" Metallica T-shirt, and a face full of acne, to one of the more popular cheerleaders. He walked to the back of the room and intercepted it before it reached her. He read it to himself: *Meet me in the church parking lot after school.*

Crumpling it up, he reprimanded them with a stern look and stuffed it in the pocket of his pants.

"Anyone?" he asked, glancing out the window at two boys running from the school as he made his way back to the front of the class. "Why would George shoot his best friend? Does this indicate that they weren't friends at all?"

A hand went up. He looked over at Gina, sitting with her shoulders back and chest sticking out, smiling up at him from her desk.

"Yes...Gina," he said. Her name was thick rolling off his tongue. His heart began to race. He took off his glasses and wiped them with his tie again.

"Because he loved Lenny," Gina said, shifting in her seat.

He became lightheaded and sat down on the corner of an empty desk. His mouth dried up. A thin layer of film covered his tongue.

"Good," he said. "Explain what you mean by that."

Gina sucked on the end of her pen as she composed a response. Again the picture of her body naked on his couch crept into his mind. He placed his hand over his face and wiped the sweat off his forehead before looking back at her.

"Well, George, like, loved Lenny. He knew Curley wanted to kill him because Lenny, like, killed his wife, but didn't really mean it. So George started telling Lenny about the rabbits and stuff, so Lenny would be happy before he died. He did it because he really was his friend and really cared about him. When you really love somebody you'll do anything for him, you know? You care about them more than you care about yourself. Even if it means doing things that you know are…wrong." Gina stared at him.

There was another long, onerous silence. A couple of sleepers lifted their heads to see what was going on. Kevin's heart continued to pound. He looked around the classroom. All eyes were focused on him. He coughed nervously and tried to put his book down on the desk he was sitting on, but it fell to the floor. He leaned over to pick it up as the bell rang.

He looked up at the class, startled. The students gathered their books and started to make their way to the door. Frazzled, he fought to get one last word in above the chatter and shuffling of desks. "Umm…very good, Gina. If you haven't finished reading *Of Mice and Men*, make sure you have it finished by tomorrow," he said in a loud voice, hoping to get the attention of the students who were already in the hallway. He placed his hands over his face and took a couple of deep breaths. He felt a finger tap his shoulder.

Gina stood in front of him with her books covering her chest. She smiled at him, reached into a notebook and pulled out a piece of paper folded neatly into a triangle.

"See you tomorrow, Mr. Cohen," she said, handing him the note and leaning over to kiss him on the cheek.

He jumped back and forced a weak smile. He walked quickly

to the chalkboard. "Yes, see you tomorrow, Gina," he said without turning to look at her.

As Gina left the classroom, Kevin sat down in the chair behind his desk and tried to gather himself for the class coming in. He unfolded the note and laid it down flat on his lap: *Can I see you tomorrow night? Let me know. Love, Gina.*

The handwriting was in neat cursive with small hearts dotting the I's.

Kevin tore the note into pieces and stuffed it in his pocket with the other one. A few students from his next class began to sit down, boisterously blabbing about a fight in the hallway.

"Eric Dorsey just got his ass kicked by D.J. Marcone, Mr. Cohen. You should've seen it," a boy in the front row said.

Kevin nodded his head. "Is that so?"

"I fucked up, man. I really fucked up." Kevin reached for his pack of cigarettes and lit one, blowing a cloud of smoke in Dan's face. He stared down into his double-scotch on the rocks.

"What d'ya mean? Did you kill Julie's new boyfriend? Cut him up in little pieces, bag him and stuff him in your freezer?" Dan smiled and took a sip from his Budweiser. It was a little past five, and the Barley House had started to fill up with businessmen just off work.

"No. I didn't kill anyone. But I really fucked up this time."

"What'd ya fuck a student or something?"

Kevin looked up at Dan, solemnly staring into his eyes, then turned his head, blowing another mouthful of smoke in the opposite direction.

Dan's eyes widened. "You didn't! You're kidding me, right? You would never...no way! You gotta be bullshitting me." Dan reached over the table and grabbed Kevin by the shirt collar, pulling him close enough to feel his breath on his face. It smelled of beer and mint chewing tobacco.

"I'm serious, man. I fucked up! I mean, really, really fucked up. I don't know what to do." Kevin flinched, bracing himself for a punch he was fairly sure Dan would never throw. Dan, a History teacher and the football coach at the high school, was considerably larger and stronger than Kevin, yet in their four years of friendship, he'd never even pushed him jokingly.

"Who is she? She's at least eighteen, right?" Dan released Kevin's shirt and shoved him back into his chair.

"No. She's sixteen. A junior," Kevin said. His voice cracked and his legs went numb.

"You stupid asshole," Dan said, staring straight into Kevin's eyes. "You realize you can go to jail if the wrong people find out, right? What were you thinking? What the fuck were you thinking sticking it in one of the students?"

Kevin didn't have an answer. They had joked about having sex with some of their attractive female students, but neither of them ever imagined it would progress beyond a lewd fantasy. Dan was married, and Kevin had always been tacitly acknowledged as the more sensible of the two. He reached into his pocket and felt the torn pieces of the note Gina had given him in class. He let the paper press against his sweaty palm. Tears welled in the corners of his eyes.

"Who was it?" Dan asked, leaning over the table.

"It's not important."

"Who was it?"

"I don't want to tell you. I think you had her in class."

"Who the fuck was it? I just want to know if it's someone who will blow the horn on you."

"Gina Parente." Saying her full name made him cringe.

Dan shook his head. "Shit, man. She's a nice girl. What the fuck were you thinking? What are you going to do? Do you think she'll tell anybody?" Dan took another slug off his beer. His eyes never left Kevin's face. He slammed the bottle down on the table and waited for a response.

"I don't think so. But she wants to see me again. Tomorrow night," Kevin said.

"You stupid son of a bitch. You aren't going to see her again, right? What are you going to do? Are you going to see her again?"

"I think I better. I mean, I think I should probably talk to her. Like you said, she's a nice girl. Not the kind of girl that would screw her teacher to brag to her friends or to get a grade. But I think she's fallen for me." Saying those words choked him. *She's fallen for me.*

"You're right. You really fucked up," Dan said, shaking his head.

Kevin lit another cigarette off the end of the one he was smoking and ordered another double-scotch on the rocks. He inhaled deeply. He could hardly believe he'd quit smoking for two and a half years.

She stood under a streetlight on Pleasant Street. Kevin watched her from his car, parked around the corner. He'd told her as she was leaving class on Friday to wait for him at 7:30. She'd smiled, blowing a kiss over her shoulder as she walked out of the classroom.

She removed a compact from her pocketbook and checked her lipstick. Her long brown hair whipped around in the cold winter breeze. She was wearing a tight black dress, a pair of black patent leather heels, and thin red cardigan. She hugged herself and shivered. From a passing glance, Kevin thought, you'd guess she was at least eighteen, if not older.

Her head perked up at each set of approaching headlights then dropped when the cars failed to stop. Kevin's stomach sank as he watched her standing there alone in the cold. She was only a girl— young, impressionable, desperately trying to seem more mature than she was. He wanted to go over to her, take her in his arms and protect her from the wind. He wanted her to tell him she'd get over it and remember him as her teacher, not some dissolute twenty-eight year old who took advantage of her during a night of carelessness. He knew this was impossible. He never wanted this to happen. He never meant to do this to Gina. She was only a girl. A girl waiting on a cold street corner for headlights to appear and a warm car to carry her away.

He started the car. He was going back to his apartment. He wondered just how long she'd wait there before leaving. Looking for someone to talk to. Someone to tell.

Kevin sat behind his desk nervously organizing papers, pens and folders, glancing at the door as the students began filtering into the classroom. He was waiting for her. After returning to his apartment Friday night, he sat down and wrote a long letter— an incriminating document. But he wrote it anyway. In it, he profusely apologized and pleaded for Gina's understanding. He kept it neatly folded in his pocket. He was going to give it to her after class. All weekend he'd prayed that she wouldn't open her mouth and the letter would resolve things.

Gina walked into the classroom. Kevin looked up. Their eyes met for a second, then they both turned away. Gina walked briskly across the room, sat down and folded her hands on her desk. Her face was expressionless.

"Okay, will everyone take out their homework from Friday," Kevin said, standing up from his desk and approaching the front of the room. "Please pass it to the front."

When he got to Gina's row, she reached back and grabbed the thin stack of papers. She handed them to Kevin with her head turned and arm outstretched.

"Thank you, Gina," he said softly.

She ignored him.

The period passed slowly. Each word out of Kevin's mouth seemed to stick on his lips before finding sound. He kept glancing at Gina while the other students took turns reading aloud from a handout of "The Chrysanthemums". He shivered when Elisa Allen found her flowers on the side of the road after being conned by the traveler. He consciously avoided a discussion of the symbolism. He looked over at Gina, who kept her eyes down and listlessly flipped through pages in her notebook.

The bell finally rang.

"Gina, can I see you for a second?" He put his hand in his pocket and clenched the letter as the class filed out into the hallway.

Gina stood in front of him, restively looking around the room. Breathing heavily. She had her books in front of her chest.

Kevin sat down on a desk, removed his glasses and wiped them with his tie. "Gina, we need to talk."

"About what?" Gina said.

Kevin took a deep breath as he removed the letter from his pocket. "About what happened," he said.

"Gina? You coming?" A voice came from the doorway. A young man stood there with his books tucked under his arm like a football. "Oh, hey, Mr. Cohen. How's it going?"

Kevin paused for a moment, stunned. "Not too bad, David. How are you doing?"

Kevin had had David Lowe in his class when he was a freshman. David was one of the more popular students—a senior athlete, conventionally handsome, the town's golden boy.

"I'm doing good. Starting to get ready for basketball season. I should make All-State this year," David said, hopping restlessly from one foot to the other like he was warming up for a fight. "Gina, you coming?"

Kevin looked at Gina, who kept her head down. "I think that's great," Kevin said to David. "That's great, Gina." He placed the letter back in his pocket.

"I gotta go," she said. "I have to get to Algebra." She pushed her way past Kevin and met David in the doorway with a long, open-mouthed kiss. Kevin watched for a second then walked to his desk. He held the letter in his pocket, let it drop and wiped his sweaty hand on the leg of his beige khakis.

"See ya later, Mr. Cohen," David said. He and Gina disappeared into the hallway commotion.

Kevin took out the letter and tore it into pieces. He looked at the scraps lying in his hand then put them back in his pocket. He felt the torn paper slipping through his fingers. He tried to smile at the first student who walked into class, but it felt wrong. Forced. He needed a cigarette. He could hardly believe he'd quit for two and a half years.

THE
BIG
GIG

I DRANK too much coffee, mostly because it was there and would've been thrown out. I hate seeing shit wasted. I had to brew a new pot every time a customer came in and complained that it was "burned" or "stale." There was a Dunkin Donuts just down the road. I always wanted to tell them to shut their damn mouths, cough up the extra fifty cents, and buy their coffee from a place that specializes in that shit. Instead, I had to look sorry, you know, raising my eyebrows like it's a big fucking shock or something, and say, "Is it really not delicious? Oh God, I'm sorry. You can have that cup for free." I hated that shit. All that hassle for a buck over minimum wage, and I wasn't about to get a raise any time soon. The owner, Jack Doyle, had such a stick up his ass he reminded me of a fucking corndog or something. Cheap bastard. I don't know what I was thinking, working the dayshift six days a week.

Anyway, I drank too much coffee. I'd finished taking inventory, counting the register, wiping the shelves and all the other crap I had to do before I could leave. I was just waiting for Lisa—a fat chick with this lame-ass tattoo of Tweetie Bird on her forearm—to show up and replace me at 5:00 p.m. I stood behind the register while the caffeine went through my veins like flames shot from a fucking furnace. Besides the shakes and generally feeling like shit, I had a lot on my mind. My band, The Shit Stains, was playing its first gig that night at Penuche's. It was all pretty cool and shit, but when we printed flyers we had to bill ourselves as *The S— Stains*, or else we couldn't hang them up downtown. No one in Concord had any balls.

We were a punk band who played a lot of old school covers, but we also played a couple of originals like "Fuck This Shitty Job" and "Blue-Collar Anarchy," which I wrote. We didn't play tunes by any of those faggot-ass pop bands like Green Day. We had actually started by playing classic rock covers, a little Zeppelin and some Floyd, then we finally woke up to punk. We were pretty old school.

There were three of us in The Shit Stains. I played the guitar, a sweet looking red Strat that I got off my older brother after he got a Les Paul with the insurance money after some old bat rear-ended him on Main St. I also sang lead. Roach played bass and sang background. His real name was Alex Rogers, but everyone called him Roach because he smoked enough weed to make Cypress Hill look like amateurs. And Stewey. Damian Stewart was our drummer, and he, well…he had his own thing going on. Nice fucking guy. Just a little bit freaky. Anyway, we really ripped shit up for three guys who never took lessons.

I was standing behind the counter waiting for Lisa to take her hand out of the Dorito bag, pull her fat ass off the couch and get into work when Roach came in. His eyes were tiny slits in his face, and he had this shit-eating smirk that he always got after pulling bong hits.

"Wassup, bitch?" he said, blowing into his hands. It was cold as hell outside.

"Nothing, man. I'm waiting for fucking fat-ass to show up," I said, tapping my fingers on the counter.

Roach was almost as tall as me when I was standing on the six-inch lift behind the counter. I'm kind of short and all, but Roach was one of those really lanky bastards with a crew cut and roots dyed blue that week. He wore his black leather jacket with all the buckles and zippers hanging off it and a red anarchy sign painted on the back.

I stood there with my chin resting in my hand, obviously pissed off and scowling and shit. It was already after 5:00 p.m. and there still wasn't any sign of Lisa. I had to stop by Nikki's place after work to get my lucky T-shirt, which I'd left over there. Nikki was my girlfriend. We started dating our sophomore year in high school and had been going together for ten years. I would've married her, but who the fuck can afford an engagement ring? Nikki was traditional like that and wanted all the bullshit that goes along with a wedding. I would've just run off to Atlantic City or something. After getting my shirt, I was going to the Hole—the place where we practiced. We had to pack our shit into Stewey's old man's van, set up for the gig, do a sound check and be ready to rip shit up by 10:00 p.m.

"What's up your ass, Pete?" Roach said, taking a Snickers bar from a rack and opening it.

"You gonna pay for that?" I asked.

Roach laughed and took a bite. "No."

"Dude, you're gonna get me fucked stealing shit like that. Now I have to pay for the fucking candy bar because your unemployed ass can't afford it." I reached in my pocket, took out a couple of quarters and dropped them in the register. I don't know why I even bothered. That job sucked anyway. And what did I give a shit if they fired my ass? I didn't.

"Dude, chill out. Remember we have a gig tonight," Roach said, finishing the Snickers bar.

"I know, man. But fucking Lisa ain't here yet, and I have to go to Nikki's place before going down to the Hole. I left my lucky T-shirt there, and I ain't playing without it," I said.

"Man, I don't know why you bother with her. How many times do I have to tell you? She's fucking Little. My kid sister's in his class right now and she heard the same thing," Roach said.

"She's not fucking Little. She wanted him to look over some of her poems or some shit like that." Nikki wrote poetry. She was really fucking good. "Just because she went over the guy's apartment doesn't mean she's fucking him."

"Dude, he's a fucking *math* teacher! Why is he reading her poems?"

"Listen, asshole, Nikki and I have been together for ten years.

I'd know if she was banging someone else. Besides, she wouldn't do that to me," I said. Nikki and I both had Little for Algebra in high school, and he didn't seem like the type who'd go around fucking ex-students and shit. In fact, most of us thought he was a fag.

"Whatever, man. I still think you're being played for a little bitch."

"Call me a bitch again, and I'll knock your fucking teeth out!" I was serious, too.

"Whatever," Roach said, picking up a Butterfinger from the shelf and putting it down before I jumped over the counter and ripped his fucking throat out. "Hey, man, Ed's coming down from Plymouth tonight. He said he'd help us move the equipment if we get him a six-pack."

This guy Ed was a complete pain in the ass. He wasn't really a bad guy, but he always moped around, whining about his ex-girlfriend. He was depressing as shit. It took about ten minutes of listening to the son of a bitch before I was ready to slit my fucking wrists.

"I'm not buying beer for him. We can move the crap ourselves," I said. I wasn't about to buy that guy a six-pack for lifting a couple of amps, which was exactly how it would go, seeing Roach didn't have a job or any cash. He lived with his folks and sold just enough weed to keep a head bag. But he never made any cash. That's the problem with potheads: they're always too burnt to figure out the simple things, like don't smoke off your own supply. Me? I stay away from weed and all that other hippie shit.

Roach ignored me. He was zoning out on a Budweiser promotional poster with a hot blonde babe in a red bikini.

I was just about to call Lisa's place when she waddled into the store. She had obviously just come from the hairdresser because her plain black hair had these flaming blond streaks in them, which made her look a little like a big stuffed zebra. I never understood why fat chicks wasted their money at beauty salons. Her lips were plastered with a thick layer of white lipstick and her small mouth was sandwiched between her doughy cheeks, like one of those old

Cabbage Patch Kids. Some big women would look good if they lost fifty pounds or so, but not Lisa. She was just fucking ugly. Hopeless. Usually I feel bad for chicks like her, but she didn't even have a good personality. She had one of those attitudes where she seemed to miss the facts: she was fat, she was ugly, and she had no right to walk around like she owned the fucking world or something.

Lisa carried this big-ass black leather purse and had on a matching black leather coat that must've taken six fucking cows to make. She took these long, exaggerated breaths. Being so big, she was always breathing heavy, but this was the intentional kind of deep breathing. Like she wanted us to know that something happened that caused her to not only breathe heavy, but also be five minutes late for work. She always tried pulling that shit when she was late.

"Sorry I'm late, but this guy at the salon wouldn't stop talking to me. I mean, I told him I was going to be late for work, but he just went on and on," she said, making yapping motions with her hands.

Bullshit, I thought. I just shook my head and didn't say anything.

Lisa looked at Roach. Her chubby cheeks stretched into this big fucking smile.

"Hi, Alex," she said, rubbing up against him like a cat does when it wants to eat.

"Hey," Roach said without looking at her. He got really smashed one night at Penuche's and ended up taking Lisa home. He denied anything happened, but Stewey and I both saw him sucking her fat face in a corner booth by the bathrooms and leaving with her afterwards. Ever since, Lisa had the idea in her head that Roach was her boyfriend. She called him at least twice a week and even baked him a fucking cake for his birthday. Roach tried to ignore her, but she just wouldn't leave him alone. She really had it in for him.

"I heard you guys are playing tonight," Lisa said, tossing one of the blond streaks off her face like she was a fucking Hollywood actress or something.

"Yeah," Roach said. Still not looking up.

"I can't wait to see you guys," she said.

"Umm...yeah. Listen, man. I gotta split," Roach said, turning to me. "I'll meet you down at the Hole about 7:00, right?"

"Yeah, I'll be down there after I get my T-shirt," I said, putting on my army field jacket and a pair of black wool gloves with the fingers cut off.

Roach bolted out of the store and disappeared around the corner before Lisa could get another word out.

"Everything should be all set," I said to Lisa. "You'll probably have to make some coffee in an hour or so."

"I don't know why these people don't just go to Dunkin Donuts," she said, taking off her coat and putting it behind the counter.

I shrugged. I reached in my coat pocket and grabbed a cigarette. "See ya later," I said.

"Yeah, good luck tonight."

"Thanks," I said. I guess she wasn't that bad.

I lit the cigarette in the store and walked outside. The cold wind hit my face like a fucking sucker punch. I walked carefully over the ice patches in front of the store. I should've thrown some sand over them, but what did I care if that cheap bastard Doyle got the shit sued out of him?

It was 5:15 according to the clock in the store. My breath and the smoke made this big cloud in front of my face. Shit, it was cold, and it felt like it was going to snow or rain or something—sort of thick and heavy air. I turned on West St. and walked by the laundromat on my way to Nikki's place.

Nikki lived with her sister, Dawn, and Dawn's husband, Tom. They had an old two-story house with the blue paint chipping off the windows and the siding and shit. Tom bought it in the early Nineties from some old bag who was sick of renting the place and wanted to move to Florida with all the other old bags. The bathrooms were small, and the ceiling on the second floor was so low you would've thought midgets lived there at some point. I always said Roach would knock his head fifty times a day walking around the place, but that would've probably done him some good.

Nikki stayed on the second floor and only paid 200 bucks a month to live there, so she never complained. She had a living-room, a bedroom and her own bathroom. Not a bad deal.

I walked right in and went up the stairs without stopping to say hello to Tom, who was watching a rerun of *Roseanne*, lying on the couch and drinking Budweiser. Tom was a plumber—one of those big, bearded biker-types who didn't say much, just grunted all the time. He wasn't a bad guy, but he hated my fucking guts for some reason. I asked Nikki once why he hated me, and she said it wasn't my fault. It was Tom. Not like I gave a flying fuck or anything.

I walked down the hallway. It was already dark, so it was a bitch to see. But I knew my way around that place like the back of my fucking hand, so I went straight to Nikki's room. The door was closed, but I knew she was home because I saw her pocketbook on the stairs. I just walked in, like I always did, thinking she might be sleeping or something and I'd wake her up by kissing her cheek and forehead and shit. Sometimes I did that romantic shit that chicks really dig.

When I opened the door, the lamp on the nightstand was on, and Nikki was laying on her back on her bed with her shirt off and a tit popped out of her bra like someone jimmied it out with a screwdriver. Leaning on his elbow with his tongue stuck in her mouth and his hand massaging her tit was Mr. Little. As soon as she noticed me, she jumped up from the bed and tucked her tit back into her bra.

"Oh my God! Pete! I...umm...I thought...you had a gig tonight," she said, standing up, grabbing a shirt from the floor and covering her tits like I'd never seen them before or something. It was my lucky fucking T-shirt too!

Little squirmed. He matted down his hair with his hands and reached for his glasses on the nightstand. "Oh my, Peter. I really didn't— "

"Shut the fuck up!" I said, pointing at him.

My legs went numb, and I had that feeling I get in dreams when my mind tells me to start fighting but none of the muscles in my body move. I felt like a heavy sack of shit. Looking at Nikki with her short blond hair all messed up from lying on the bed and her big blue eyes looking down at the floor, I thought I was going to fucking puke. Her lips were wet with Little's spit. Or maybe I just imagined that.

Little sat on the edge of the bed, staring up at me. He looked like any middle-aged fucking nerd would look when caught holding some other guy's girlfriend's tit. His tie was loosened. His leg shook and rattled the floor.

We stayed in the same positions for a couple of seconds, all quiet and shit. I took a couple of deep breaths, thinking about lighting a cigarette and trying to calm down a bit. Then I looked at Nikki and thought I was going to start bawling or something. I had one of those lumps in my throat that made it hard to swallow.

"I came for my T-shirt," I said.

"Listen Pete, it's not what you think," Nikki said, still staring at the floor.

"Fuck you, it's not what I think! What is it then? Was he reading more of your poems?"

Little sat on the edge of the bed wringing his hands. I could see a bald spot on the top of his head where his hair parted. I wanted to fucking kill him.

"I'm sorry, Pete. It's just that— "

"Fuck you, Nikki! Ten years, man. Ten fucking years!" I didn't know what else to say. I felt like leaping over the bed, grabbing Little by the neck and ripping his fucking throat out. But I didn't. I just stood there. Like a bitch.

Nikki didn't say anything.

"Can I have my T-shirt?" I asked. I tried to sound tough, but that lump in my throat, man, it made my voice crack and sound all weepy and shit.

Nikki handed me the T-shirt. I felt like I was going to puke again, so I turned around and slammed the door behind me. I sprinted down the hallway then down the stairs. As I opened the front door, I could hear Tom in the living room, laughing. Fuck him.

I ran to the side of the house, leaned over by a bush and puked three good mouthfuls of the stale coffee that had been sitting in my gut. The blood vessels in my face seemed about to pop. I dry-heaved a couple of times, stood up straight and steadied myself.

I stood by the bush, wiping my eyes with the palms of my hands. I began walking, unsure of what direction I was heading. Everything had happened so fast that I felt dizzy and sort of drunk. I looked up and noticed there were no stars out that night.

I found myself wandering under the streetlights on South State St. My hands were buried in my coat pockets. I was looking at the sidewalk as I walked. I couldn't think of anything really, but I was thinking about everything at the same time.

I looked up at the sky. The moon stuck out a little from behind some dark clouds, but I still couldn't see any stars. I wished, maybe even convinced myself that it was one of those fucked up dreams where you wake up and you're so fucking grateful that it really didn't happen. A picture of Little snuggling up to Nikki after I left went through my head like a fucking spike. I could see his hand reaching around and popping out her tit again, saying, "I'm sorry Nikki." I wondered if she would finish him off after that. Maybe she'd slip her hand into his pants and jerk him off. Or maybe she would put his little dick in her mouth and suck him until he blew it down her throat. I couldn't take it. I just kept walking.

I ended up turning onto Pleasant St. and standing in front of the building where I was supposed to meet the guys. It was a video store, and the Hole was in the basement. I just stood outside shivering. Then I balled my fist and got ready to punch the side of the building. But I looked down and noticed I was still carrying my lucky T-shirt. It was an old 1986 Motley Crue "Girls, Girls, Girls" tour shirt with the band in their biker clothes on the front— it was during the stage where Motley Crue ditched the hairspray and makeup for that grungy biker look. On the back was a list of tour dates. It was originally my older brother Rick's shirt. He actually saw the show in Boston, but he gave it to me when I was in junior high. I wore it to school the day I asked Nikki out for the first time. Vince Neil's and Mick Mars' faces were just about washed away, and the tour dates on the back were faded and flaked, but some things I just can't throw away. I mean, I'm not really sentimental and shit. But this shirt had some memories attached to it.

I looked down at the shirt and realized if I'd hit the wall, I could've broken my fucking hand. I needed it to play the guitar. Then I snapped out of it. I didn't have time to let myself get all fucked up over a girl. The Shit Stains, the band that was about to recreate punk rock, was playing its first gig in less than four hours.

I raised my fist to the sky and screamed, "Fucking right!"

I was only a few blocks from my brother's house, where I lived with his wife and two kids. I wasn't making enough dough to live on my own. I thought of taking a shower but decided to skip it and go straight down to the Hole smelling like puke and cigarettes. Someday I'd talk about that in an interview for *Rolling Stone*: "Yeah, at my first gig, I smelled like puke and shit, but I didn't give a fuck. I knew the show had to go on…"

I walked into the video store and waved to Christina, this cute high school chick who worked there. She waved back with her fingertips, giggling and blushing. She had perfect posture, like a lot of those young girls. She reminded me a little bit of Nikki when she was in high school—all her parts so new and tight. I watched Nikki's posture start to sag over ten years, like watching mold grow on cheese or some shit like that. Don't get me wrong, Nikki still had great posture, but she didn't have the same stuff that Christina had anymore. I turned right at the entrance and opened the door that went down the stairs into the Hole.

I took out my keys, opened the door and was slapped in the fucking face by the stench of weed. Roach was already down there. There was a small message board by the door and a calendar that listed gigs and rehearsal times for the bands that practiced there. We shared the space with two others bands: Dark Star, a bunch of fucking hippies who played Grateful Dead and Phish covers in the bars around Concord, and Hot Damn!, my brother Rick's band. They had a real bluesy base to them, but in order to get gigs, they had to sell out and play popular covers like "Sweet Home Alabama," "Feel Like Making Love" and the bullshit you hear on the radio these days. They were starting to do weddings and bringing in some decent cash. They were older guys with families and shit and they needed the dough.

On the bottom of the board was that weak-ass flyer we were hanging around town: *The S— Stains, Penuche's, Friday, March 7th 10:00 p.m..*

I could hear Roach plucking away at his bass. I walked in, still carrying my lucky T-shirt. The Hole was pretty much a fucking dive—a dark, large, open space with three drum kits set up in different corners of the room. A beat-up couch and a dartboard were in the left corner from the entrance. There weren't any windows, seeing it was a basement. The place stunk of mold, stale cigarettes, and weed. White blinking Christmas lights were strung up on the walls. The walls and the ceiling were insulated with egg crates to keep the sound from disturbing the customers in the video store. The place kind of sucked, but it was a cheap place to practice, so we never bitched.

Roach was sitting in a wooden chair by Stewey's drum kit. His friend Ed stood next to him, lighting a bowl. Ed was one of those guys whose bottom lip was too big for his fucking face. He had these droopy sad-sack eyes and his whole face had this downward slope to it, like he'd spent too much time crying into a pillow and it just got stuck that way. He took a hit and passed the bowl to Roach.

I walked over without saying a word to either of them and sat down on the drum stool.

Roach put down his bass and held out the bowl to me.

"Get that fucking hippie shit away from me," I said. I used to smoke weed, but then it started making me paranoid. I was already feeling fucking edgy enough.

Roach shrugged, took a hit and passed the bowl back to Ed.

"Someone's on the rag today," Roach said, coughing out a large cloud of smoke.

"Shut the fuck up," I said. I wasn't sure if I wanted to mention

Nikki and Little or not.

"How's it going?" Ed asked.

"Not bad," I said. "How's it going with you?"

"Same old shit. Cindy and Steve are thinking of moving in together, so I may not have a place to live next month," Ed said. His face sunk lower with each word out of his mouth. His misery was almost enough to cheer me up.

"That sucks," I said. I didn't want to pry any further with questions. I knew he was waiting for one so he could go off on the topic and I'd be stuck listening to stories about Steve and Cindy (who I didn't know from a fucking hole in the wall) for the rest of the night. He cornered me one night a couple of months before, and I swear I was going to blow off my fucking head if I heard anything else about Steve, Cindy or how the poor son of a bitch had to listen to them screwing. Even Roach knew better.

"When's Stewey supposed to show?" I turned to Roach.

"I think he said," Roach coughed, "7:00, but I'm not sure. He had to work until 6:30."

"Is he still doing the raincoat thing?" I asked.

At that time Stewey was wearing raincoats everywhere, and not those somewhat trendy long trench coats. He wore one of those mid-length, bright banana yellow raincoats with a hood and walnut-sized buttons. Stewey had these "phases" where he'd start doing something that didn't make sense to anyone in the world, but to Stewey it was natural, like breathing. For example, before the raincoat, he memorized three or four Dr. Seuss books, and when anyone would have a conversation with the fucking guy, he'd just throw random *Cat In The Hat* or *Green Eggs and Ham* quotes at them. It was fucking weird. No one could understand it. It wasn't like he wanted attention or did a lot of drugs—just a little weed after rehearsals and occasionally some speed. When I asked him what was up with the raincoat in the middle of winter he just said, "You never know when it will rain." That was it. I dropped the issue. Weird shit. But he was a good fucking drummer.

"The last I saw him he was wearing the raincoat and that was earlier today when I went looking for a job," Roach said, taking another hit.

"You didn't go looking for any fucking job," I said. Roach's idea of looking for a job was going to the gas station where Stewey worked to talk to him, asking him if they had any positions available and *maybe* filling out an application, but never turning it in.

"Whatever, man. But yeah, he was still wearing the raincoat," Roach said, passing the bowl to Ed.

I looked up at the string of blinking lights around the room. "I caught Little holding Nikki's tit a little while ago," I said. I don't know why I said it, I just did.

"What!" Roach's eyes widened.

"Yeah, you were right, man. She was making a bitch of me."

"Aw, shit, man. I'm sorry. I didn't really mean...you know. I'm sorry, man," Roach said. Then he looked me in the eyes for one of the first times since I'd known him. I just shrugged and grinned. He was a really good bass player.

"Believe me, I know how you feel," Ed said. "One time I walked in on Steve eating Cindy out." He passed the bowl back to Roach, who puffed on it, then tapped it out on his Doc Marten.

I had the lucky T-shirt hanging out the back of my jeans like I was some Bruce Springsteen "Born In The U.S.A." asshole. I decided to change.

I took off my coat and the shirt I was wearing and put on the lucky T-shirt. It fit snugly around my gut, which was getting big from too many nights sucking back drafts at Penuche's. But it felt good. It felt like I'd become someone else. Like a fucking rock star.

I grabbed a can of Bud Light from the refrigerator underneath the dartboard. We were waiting for Stewey. It was already 7:30 and I was starting to get really pissed off. Here it was our first gig, the night everything was supposed to fall into place and The Shit Stains were going to begin kicking ass on the Concord music scene, and Stewey was late. And we couldn't move our shit without his old man's van.

Roach and Ed kept packing bowls and passing them back and forth without saying anything. Roach considered himself something like a Rastafarian and even tried growing dreadlocks a couple of years before, but he ended up looking like a Q-tip that blew up at the end.

Finally at 7:45, Stewey showed up in his yellow raincoat, a plain white T-shirt and a pair of dark blue Wrangler jeans. He had his head shaved and was wearing horn-rimmed glasses. He was wiry, but muscular from doing 50 push-ups and 100 sit-ups every morning. I watched him one morning at my place, doing these push-ups and sit-ups and shit. He never missed them, no matter how fucking hungover he was.

He walked up to us without saying a word and started packing his bass drum into its black canvas case.

I watched him for a few seconds, shaking my head. "Where the fuck have you been? I hope you have a good fucking excuse! The gig starts in less than two and a half hours, and we don't even have the shit packed yet. What about a sound check? What about setting up? Where the fuck where you?"

Ed and Roach stood in the corner looking up at the Christmas lights. Stewey turned to me and shrugged. The plastic on the yellow raincoat cracked in the silence. "I was taking a bath," he said.

He looked at me like there was nothing weird about taking a long bath on the most important night of his life.

"You were what? Taking a goddamn, motherfucking, son of a bitching bath while we waited here for you?"

Stewey nodded his head and started unscrewing his high hat. "I was dirty."

"Why would you take such a long bath, yet wear a goddamn raincoat all the time to keep from getting wet?"

"Oh, no," Stewey said, all calm and shit, "I wore the raincoat."

"In the bath?" Roach asked.

"Yeah," Stewey said, and continued packing his kit like that was completely fucking normal.

We all looked at one another then started laughing our fucking balls off, except for Stewey who just shrugged his shoulders. At that moment, in that cellar, under the Christmas lights, The Shit Stains were about to start kicking some *serious* ass. A fucking freight train couldn't have taken us out. I pictured us sitting in a hot tub, surrounded by porn stars with their long nails massaging my scalp, while I flipped through a copy of *Rolling Stone* with our faces on the fucking cover. We laughed, not just at Stewey's bath, but at the whole fucking asshole world that had been keeping us down in a basement for so long. I pumped my fist.

"Fucking right!" I yelled.

We lugged the last amp into Stewey's old man's van—a beaten down brown piece of shit with *Stewart's Plumbing* painted on the side. It was parked on the street outside the video store. I checked the Hole for anything we may have forgotten: a distortion petal, guitar picks or cords. We had everything. Ed arranged it all in the back of the van so nothing would slide around and break on the short drive down the street to Penuche's. I guess he was pretty good at it. I mean, once he was busy with something, he didn't really talk about the ex-girlfriend and became a pretty good guy.

We stood outside the van under a streetlight, blowing on our hands and looking up at the night sky. We all lit cigarettes and had a smoke because Stewey's old man didn't want us smoking in his van. I started thinking about Nikki and how I always pictured her being at my first gig, standing in front of me while we played "Anarchy in the U.K.," which was one of her favorite songs. Something in me hoped she would show up, although I wasn't counting on it. I wiped a snot on the sleeve of my coat.

After finishing our cigarettes, we got into the van. Stewey started it up.

"Okay, last time. Do we have everything?" I asked.

"You checked, man," Roach said.

"Do you have a spare set of drumsticks?"

Stewey nodded, the yellow raincoat crackling as he put up the hood.

"Do you have an extra set of strings?" I asked Roach.

"Yeah, everything but an E, which I changed the other day. That string is nearly impossible to break anyway, man," Roach said.

"Let's go then," I said.

As we pulled out into the street, it began to sprinkle—a cold rain mixed with ice. I looked at Stewey, who flipped on the wipers and smiled.

"See. I told you," he said.

The entrance to Penuche's was in a back alley behind a bridal shop by a dumpster. We pulled the van by the dumpster, and the four of us lugged the equipment down another flight of stairs into another fucking basement. It occurred to me as I was carrying Stewey's snare drum down the stairs that we were like a breed of human rats living below the surface of society, breathing smoky air in basements and remaining hidden from the fuckers who lived above—the same people who wore ties to work and had comfortable jobs in offices. The people who went on ski weekends in the winter and barbequed in their fucking backyards in the summer and talked about shit like stocks and politics and the education system. We were different. We were ignored in our cellars, where we prepared for our strike to the surface. And one day we'd explode from below, a band of human rats with sharpened teeth and spit, beer and blood dripping from our mouths. We'd ride our power chords up to their pretty fucking surface—the shit-stained rats striking—and fuck things up when we arrived. This is only the beginning, I thought. Our first gig. Our first strike.

I stood there with the snare drum, blocking the entrance to the bar itself. Penuche's didn't have any windows or real ventilation. It smelled of stale beer and piss from the plugged shitter in the men's bathroom—the nastiest shitter in Concord. The bar itself had been rebuilt when Billy Downs bought the place a few years before from a couple who moved north to Lincoln to run a motel or something. Like any basement beer dive, it had the feel of a cave. There was a bar against the far wall and a big fucking mirror behind it. Since they didn't serve any food, Penuche's could only sell beer and wine—one of those stupid-ass New Hampshire laws. Tables, chairs and a few booths were set up around the place. There was a clearing in the corner to the right of the entrance next to a dartboard where we were going to play.

It was 8:00 p.m. The place was empty except for Sparky, a townie barfly who spent all his time hopping from bar to bar as each one shut him off. Sparky had worked as a dishwasher in every restaurant in town at some point and had been fired from every one of them as well. People said he came back from Vietnam in the mid-Seventies all fucked up. He never really talked to anyone unless he was good and loaded. He had long gray hair and one of those straggly beards that he never trimmed. He sat there on a stool at the bar, sipping a beer, mumbling to himself. I waved to him. He lifted his chin. I could tell he didn't know who the fuck I was.

Roach came up behind me and tapped me on the shoulder. Ed was standing behind him, carrying my amp.

"Man, there's nobody here," Roach said.

"It's early, man. You know nobody starts coming on Friday until at least 9:00," I said. I was a little worried though. Most of the regulars usually walked to the bar because they'd all lost their licenses after getting bagged for DWI ten fucking times or something. They were usually there by 7:00 p.m.

"Dude, this is going to be just like rehearsal, but in a different place," Roach said.

"Shut the fuck up! People are gonna come. My brother said he'd come, and Lisa said she was coming."

"Fuckin' great, man. Family and fat chicks," Roach said, walking to the corner and setting down the guitar cases.

Stewey walked in with the hood of his raincoat up. "I'm going to pull the van onto the street," he said. "Is that everything?"

I scanned the equipment—the cords, petals, microphones, amps. "Yeah, I think so. Double-check the van, man. We better start setting up," I said, walking over to the corner to help Roach and Ed unpack. I looked at a colored paper flyer taped to the wall next to a dartboard: *The S— Stains, Penuche's, Friday, March 7th 10:00 p.m.* I touched the flyer with my fingers and sighed. Someday, I thought, this is going to be a piece of rock history. The Shit Stains' first gig. Someday I'd be sitting poolside with a margarita in my hand and the porn stars on each side of me, and I'd remember this first gig playing to old Sparky and Billy Downs. I'd laugh with the guys about it, while we got fucking bombed and blown.

I could hear the rain coming down on the street above. I pulled a cigarette from my pack and lit it. I imagined the smoke rising to the surface, where those fuckers laughed at human rats, considered us filth not fit for their world and choked on our smoke. I slapped my palm against the wall. "Fucking right," I said softly, more to myself than anyone else.

I walked over to the bar and sat down at a stool. Billy Downs came over. He was a younger guy in his early thirties with a wide face and red cheeks. He had a patch of hair under his bottom lip and wore one of those gray cab driver hats backwards. He shook my hand.

"It's kinda slow tonight, man. But it should pick up," he said. He had a high voice like someone kicked him square in the nuts and he never got over it.

"No problem. We're ready to jam. 10:00, right?"

"Yeah, whenever you're ready."

"Do we get free beers for playing?"

Billy rubbed the patch of hair and pursed his lips, closing his eyes to make it seem like he was really fucking thinking about it. "Yeah, that shouldn't be a problem. Who's the other guy with you?"

"That's Ed, one of Roach's friends. He's helping us lug our shit around," I said. A loud crash came from the corner.

"What the fuck was that?" I said turning to see Roach and Ed looking down at the stack of amplifiers they'd just knocked over. The two of them stood there with their mouths opening and closing like a pair of retarded fish.

Roach looked up. "We dropped the amps, man," he said.

The amps were fine except for a small dent on the corner of mine. But I still gave Roach and Ed shit for being so fucking clumsy. Maybe if they didn't smoke until their fucking brains were toast, things like dropping amps wouldn't happen.

It was almost 9:30, and the bar was still empty except for Sparky and a few locals who worked at the paper mill in Bow. I could tell they worked at the mill by the color of their hands. The skin was slightly darker, a dirt color. They paid no attention while we went through a half-assed sound check, adjusting the amps, the microphones and tuning our guitars. Roach played his bass strings like he was brushing off a fucking eyelash or something. He was getting on my nerves by that point.

We finished the sound check and sat down at the bar to have a few beers before going on. Seeing no one showed up, not even my fucking brother, I didn't feel nervous, although I had a small cramp in my stomach. But I figured that had more to do with Nikki than the gig.

I started thinking about a day last spring when I borrowed my brother's car, and Nikki and I drove up to the Old Man on the Mountain in the Franconia Notch. We parked in one of those fucking scenic view areas off the interstate, where you could see the entire granite profile of the Old Man and snap pictures and shit if you felt like it. On the hood of the old Buick, we drank Coors Light out of McDonald's cups to keep the fucking park rangers from hassling us. Nikki leaned her head against my arm and rubbed my thigh, not in a sexual way, but another way. That afternoon there wasn't a cloud in the whole fucking sky. It looked like someone took a brush and painted the inside of an egg blue. I felt like we were sitting on the dirt gathered at the bottom of the egg and looking up. It was really corny and shit, and it probably didn't make any else to anyone other than me, but I tried to explain it to Nikki anyway. I told her how I hated being stuck in the dirt looking up, and how someday the band would make it big and me and her would be living someplace much better than the dirt and the cellars and the basements that always stunk of smoke and mold and shit. We'd get away from the drunks, potheads, dickhead bosses, and all the other stupid fuckers in Concord. I was going to be closer to the top of the fucking egg because that's the only place where someone who isn't happy being in the dirt can be. I told her to stick with me, because even though I was just a fucking convenience store clerk, I was going places. Nikki kissed me on the ear and told me she'd wait forever. She told me not to worry about it because she didn't care whether I was a clerk or a fucking rock star. And she kissed my ear again. Next thing I knew, we both had our pants off in the backseat of my brother's car. That's how it was with us. That's how I remember shit.

I sipped my beer and wished that Nikki would show up. I wanted her to see me up in front of people, singing and crunching some power chords. I couldn't get *her* out of my mind. Then, like there was some freaky psychic shit going on or something, I felt a tap on the back of my shoulder. I turned around, all excited and shit.

It was Lisa.

When I saw her wearing her big leather jacket, a tight red sweater and a pair of jeans that seemed painted to her fat ass, I looked the other way and sighed.

"Aren't you even going to say hi?" she said, leaning over my shoulder.

"Hey," I said, taking a drag off my cigarette.

"Aren't you guys supposed to be starting soon?" Lisa said, pushing one of those blond streaks off her meatball face. "There's no one here."

"Are you shitting me? There's no one here?" I turned and put my hand over my mouth like I was shocked and shit. "Fuck me, I thought the place was packed. Thanks for clearing that up for me, Lisa." I exhaled in her face.

"You don't have to be such an asshole," she said. She turned to Roach, sitting next to me shooting the shit with Ed. "Hi Alex."

"Hey," Roach said, keeping his back turned.

"Who's your friend?" she asked, smiling at Ed.

"Ed," Roach said over his shoulder.

"Hello, Ed," Lisa said, reaching her hand over Roach's back to shake hands with him.

"Hey," Ed said, waving at her. She pulled her fat hand back.

"I was going to get here earlier, but this guy Glen called me and wanted to go to a movie. I told him I couldn't because I promised you guys I'd come to your gig. Aren't you happy I showed up?" She closed her eyes, tipped back her head and crossed her hands over her chest, like she was a fucking present that we needed to unwrap.

"Thrilled," I said in a flat voice. I couldn't believe Lisa expected us to believe all of that bullshit about these guys wanting her. I felt kind of bad when I thought about it. I mean, I couldn't imagine my whole life being based around shit I made up.

Billy came up to us from behind the bar.

"Hey, guys. You may want to start soon. It's past 10:00," he said, pointing to his wrist.

"All right," I said. I looked at Roach, who scanned the bar and shrugged his shoulders. Stewey, sitting on the end, was watching a fly-fishing show on the television. "Stewey, you ready, man?"

"Dude, check this guy out. Watch him cast this thing, then snap! Pull it right back up. This is where it's at, man," Stewey said.

"Yeah, that's cool, but we're about to go on. You ready?"

"Yeah. Sure. Let's do it." Stewey stood up from his stool and practiced the fly-fishing cast with his wrists.

Billy dimmed all the lights except the one in the corner. No one seemed to notice. One of the mill workers picked his nose and flicked the snot at his friend.

We walked to the corner, under the ceiling light. Roach and I picked up our guitars, and Stewey sat down on his drum stool.

I turned on my amp and plugged in my guitar. The feedback made this piercing, screeching noise. I loved that fucking sound! I gripped the neck of my guitar like I was a holding a shotgun. Roach kicked on his amp and the microphones. Stewey stepped on the bass drum. The beat thumped in my chest. Roach strummed a few open E notes and adjusted the sound on his amp. I stepped up to the microphone.

"Is it all right back there, Billy?"

Billy gave me the thumbs up. I could see Ed and Lisa sitting on their stools. Sparky staring down in his beer. And the mill workers lined up in identical positions with both elbows on the bar and their right hands gripping their mugs.

I played a series of power chords and killed some of the feedback. I looked at Roach. A small smile formed around the edges of his mouth. My armpits started to sweat, and I could feel a fresh layer of pit juice dripping down my lucky T-shirt. I took a deep breath and closed my eyes. This was it. With our first note we'd launch out of this cellar—the shit-stained rats carrying an airborne virus to the surface, leaving all the fuckers above grasping their stomachs in pain. I stepped up to the microphone.

"One, two, three, four..."

We broke into the intro of "Blitzkrieg Bop"—a song we all agreed was recognizable enough to grab the crowd's attention yet hard enough to let them know we weren't fucking around. The power chords roared from my guitar. The rhythm pounded at my ribs. Roach and I stepped up to our microphones.

Hey, Ho, Let's go. Hey, Ho, Let's go. Hey, Ho, Let's go....

We jumped back in with the guitars—a fucking assault of distortion.

They're forming in a straight line.

The rats lined up, getting ready to climb from the cellar.

They're going through a tight wind.

Rapists plunging out of the dark, switchblades in our hands. Young women screaming, clutching their chests. The men taking cover in the streets.

The kids are losing their minds.

Flump. Thud.

Blitzkrieg Bop! I sang alone.

The drums and bass stopped. Then I stopped and turned around. Roach stood there looking down at a broken bass string. Stewey placed his drumsticks down on the floor and pulled the hood of his raincoat over his head.

"What the fuck just happened?" I asked.

"My E string, man. It broke. I don't have another one. I mean, how the fuck can I break the E? It must've been defective or something." Roach pinched the end of the snapped string and held it up. It lay in his fingers like the tail of a dead rat.

"What the fuck! You're fucking kidding me, right? Jesus Christ! Fuck! Fuck! Fuck!" I couldn't control myself. I spiked my guitar down on the floor. In one second, it had ended. All of it.

Without turning around, I just about sprinted to the fucking bar and sat down on the stool next to Lisa. Billy came up to me.

"What happened? You guys sounded all right. Why'd you stop?" Billy asked.

Lisa and Ed sat beside me with their heads down, sipping their beers.

"I'll tell you what happened. That dipshit broke his E string, and he doesn't have an extra one! First gig, and that stupid motherfucker not only broke a string that it's nearly impossible to fucking break, but he didn't bring an extra one. The gig's over, unless you have one laying around."

Billy shrugged. "No, man. We can wait and see if anyone comes in who may have one. Or I can try to call someone."

"Fuck it! Gig's over. We're finished." I didn't even want to talk about it. I was so fucking pissed off. "Can I have a beer? Bud Light."

I knew at that moment that I would never speak to Roach again. I shot a nasty look at his stupid, useless friend Ed, who got up and made his way over to the other guys. I didn't bother to turn around and watch them pack. I was finished. The band was finished. The rats were dead.

Billy put a beer in front of me. "That's $2.50, man," he said.

I looked at him, confused. Then reached in my pocket and pulled out a crumpled twenty dollar bill, flattened it out and handed it to him.

It was nearly 1:00. Last call. The guys had packed up their equipment, loaded it into the van by themselves and left shortly after we stopped. When they tried to approach me, I ignored them. I didn't ever want to see those two fucking guys again. My amp and guitar were still in the corner where I left them.

Lisa stuck around and drank with me. I told her all about Nikki and Little, and how I'd walked in on them and puked on the bush and all that shit. She listened and rubbed my back. We were both smashed when I turned to her and ran my hand through a blond streak.

"I can see why all those guys like you," I said. "You're very pretty. Did I ever tell you that?"

Lisa smiled—a large, doughy smile that looked forced. "You're just saying that because you're drunk."

"No, I mean it. You're beautiful."

"Really?"

I nodded my head.

"Do you want to go somewhere and talk?" I kind of knew what I was saying, but I didn't really know why.

"I don't think I should—"

"No. Just as friends. I need a friend tonight," I said, thinking it wouldn't take much to talk Lisa into fooling around with me.

"Okay," she said.

We finished our drinks. I extended my hand to her, and she put her chubby fingers in my palm. I looked at the Tweetie Bird tattoo on her forearm and smiled. I led her from the bar up the stairs. We walked out into the cold rain.

CATCH

KERRI took the brush in her left hand and with a careful stroke painted a purple circle around her right nipple. She needed to feel the brush pressed against a surface. She giggled to herself and painted her left nipple as well. She stood in front of the canvas in a pair of plain white panties with one hand resting on her bony hip, the other holding the brush in front of her. Looking out the window of her small studio apartment, she watched a couple walk out of the Barley House onto Main Street, which was deserted like rest of downtown Concord on a Thursday afternoon. Dark clouds had gathered above the golden dome of the New Hampshire State House. A sullen mist and patches of gray fog hovered over the sidewalks. A meter officer wrote out a ticket and placed it authoritatively on the windshield of a Ford pickup. Life as usual in the sleepy state capitol.

Kerri sighed, running her hand through her short, black hair. She hadn't sold a painting in six months, and it was beginning to seem like her job at The Coffee Mill was destined to become more than a temporary source of income. Nikki, her only real friend in Concord, told her that most artists start with the intention of becoming a painter, musician or writer and end up as waitresses, retail clerks or shift managers somewhere. Nikki knew because she herself wrote poetry and worked with Kerri at the café. Following a discouraging creative writing class and an onslaught of rejection letters, Nikki decided to stop writing, claiming that no one was willing to give her a fair chance. However, she still read at an open-mic night once a week at the Café Eclipse in front of a familiar crowd who seemed to like her poetry.

Kerri walked away from the canvas. She could never *really* get away from it. It lurked in her peripheral vision no matter where she moved in the apartment. She picked up a navy blue men's dress shirt that was tossed over the back of the couch—one of the many things James conspicuously left in her apartment after their breakup. It was his way of trying to make his presence linger in her life. It didn't work. James was the most recent boyfriend, and before him there was Mike, and before him Stephen, and before him Plato—a street musician in Boston that she dated for the simple, cryptic reason that he called himself "Plato".

She rolled up the sleeves of the shirt and buttoned it halfway, covering her purple nipples. James was a big man. But for a big man, he didn't have any thrust. That's what Kerri remembered about him, if she remembered anything at all.

She lay down on the couch, lit a cigarette and exhaled, watching the smoke slowly rise to the low ceiling. The telephone rang. She briefly thought about answering it, but there was no one she could think of that she really *needed* to talk to. She let the answering machine pick it up.

"Hey beautiful." A deep voice came from the machine sitting on the counter that separated the living room from the kitchen. Kerri placed her cigarette between her lips and covered her ears with her hands. She waited until she heard a faint beep before uncovering them again.

She knew she was beautiful. Businessmen, lawyers and politicians from the State House reminded her daily when they came into the café at lunch, wearing expensive suits, ordering deli sandwiches and mineral waters, and dropping ten dollar bills and napkins with their cell phone numbers shamelessly into the tip jar. She knew she was beautiful and sometimes wished she wasn't. She wished she could go to bars and have a beer without men who stunk of cologne trying to buy her drinks and bombarding her with bad pick-up lines. She wanted to be taken seriously as an artist and a woman. Sometimes she looked in the mirror and examined her slim, bronze-skinned figure for any imperfection that would make her less of a beautiful woman and more of a serious artist. She'd search for cellulite, lip hair, all the things most women detested.

She crushed her cigarette in the ashtray, grabbed a pillow by her feet and placed it underneath her head. While watching a patch of fog brush by the large window behind the canvas, she fell asleep.

She awoke to a buzzing noise. She looked tiredly around her dark apartment, rubbing her eyes. She glanced at the alarm clock on the small night table by her bed. She had slept over five hours. The buzzing continued—incessant and piercing. Kerri reached over and turned on the lamp by the couch. She lifted herself up and walked over to the intercom system on the wall.

"Who is it?" she said, her voice groggy and irritable.

"Buzz me in, Kerri. I'm coming up with a friend," Nikki said.

Kerri buzzed her in and walked over to her bed. She slipped on a pair of jeans that had been lying on the floor and fastened a few more buttons of her shirt to cover her whole chest. She knew Nikki's friend would be a man. Since breaking up with her boyfriend, Nikki had attempted to compensate for the men she'd missed out on for the past ten years by picking up everything that came her way. She was proud of her newfound promiscuity. She labeled *herself* a "slut" and found liberation in the fact that she could use men without the strain of the double standard.

Kerri pulled a cigarette from her pack and lit it as she walked to the door to unlock it. She went into the kitchen, grabbed a wine glass from the cupboard and poured herself a Merlot from an open bottle on the counter.

Nikki came in without knocking. She was followed by a tall man with broad, angular shoulders and cropped brown hair. Kerri flashed him a weak, forced smile. He was conventionally good-looking, like someone out of a J. Crew catalog. But certainly not Kerri's type.

"Kerri, this is Ryan. I met him at the Dave Matthews show the other night. Ryan, this is my friend, Kerri," Nikki said, placing a brown paper bag on the floor.

Ryan extended a large hand. Kerri, switching her wine glass from her right hand to her left, shook his hand firmly.

"It's nice to meet you, Kerri," he said. Kerri could sense the motive in his stare, like animals sense thunderstorms. He was translucent and predictable. She pulled her hand away and turned her back to him.

Nikki glanced at the wine glass in Kerri's hand. "Good, you started without us," she said, removing two large bottles of cheap Chablis from the paper bag. She walked into the kitchen and pulled two more glasses from the cupboard. Kerri sat down in her old sofa chair, leaving the couch open for Ryan and Nikki. Ryan stared at Kerri.

The blank canvas sat on the easel in front of the window, the paints and brushes on a small table beside it. Glancing over at the canvas, Kerri wished she hadn't taken the five-hour nap. She tried to envision a picture on the canvas. Colors spun and slowly began to focus. The picture was cut off by a sharp heat on her fingers, snapping her into the reality of a cigarette burning down to its filter and into her flesh. She tossed it in the ashtray.

Ryan and Nikki sat on the couch with wine glasses in their hands. Both smiled at Kerri.

"Nikki tells me you're an artist," Ryan said, pointing toward the easel.

"When she's not brewing coffee," Nikki said, winking at Kerri.

Kerri smiled wryly. She raised her glass to her lips and took a long slug, swishing it around in her mouth before letting it slide down her throat. "I'm going to put on some music," Kerri said, standing up from her seat.

The silence in the room was oppressive. As she walked to the small portable stereo on the counter, she stumbled a little over her own feet. Her coordination was slightly affected by the quick glass of wine. She stuck a Grateful Dead bootleg into the tape deck and poured herself another glass, finishing the bottle of Merlot.

"Hey, not bad. A girl who listens to the Dead," Ryan said, picking up on the lick in "One More Saturday Night". He struck Kerri as the type of guy that went to a Dead show in college, took as many drugs as possible and bought the greatest hits album the next week.

"I told you she was something," Nikki said, placing her hand on Ryan's thigh. "I need a refill." Nikki poured herself another glass, slugged it back and poured another.

Kerri sat back down and stared at the canvas on the other side of the room. She ignored Ryan and Nikki, who started pecking at each other's lips. She was lost in the blankness of the canvas. Then the colors started spinning, and a picture worked its way into focus. She savored the fact that she could lose herself in an illusion, escape from the mundane into a place where her physical body meant nothing. The only thing of significance was the picture itself—the images and the colors slowly forming perfection. A perfection ruined by the first stroke of her brush. She ruined the picture with her hands. She made it imperfect. Slowly, the colors faded, and the picture disappeared before she could catch it.

"Kerri?" Nikki snapped her fingers. "You still with us, girl?"

Kerri looked at Ryan and Nikki molded together on the couch. She smiled at them. Nodded. She grabbed the bottle of Chablis Nikki had placed on the coffee table and refilled her glass without bothering to rinse it out. Ryan's eyes burned on her flesh, even as Nikki continued to rub his thigh, inching her hand toward the bulge in the crotch of his jeans.

Kerri let her head fall back, pulling another cigarette from her pack.

"So what do you think?" Nikki asked. "Should we order a pizza?"

"Let's just drink," Kerri said.

"Fine with me," Nikki said, and drank down another glass.

Within an hour, Nikki started stumbling to and from the bathroom, ranting and slurring about the café being a metaphor for her creative imprisonment. Kerri had heard that same speech at least a dozen drunken times before and tried to tune it out, nodding her head. Once Nikki had stopped rubbing Ryan's thigh in order to deliver her poetic manifesto, he'd lost all interest in her. He sat quietly on the couch, trying to catch Kerri's eye.

"And the white man's canon! Those boring, chauvinistic old fucks wouldn't know a good poem if it bit them in the ass," Nikki said, biting her forearm for emphasis.

"And editors today don't know good poetry from stinking piles of shit! That's why I'm not published! Well, for two reasons. The first being: society imprisons me in that goddamn stupid café... are you guys listening?" She pointed at Ryan, then Kerri.

They both nodded.

"Good. Because I'm serious. This is important. The second reason nobody publishes me is because the literary world wouldn't know good writing if it fucked them. I'm going to end up like Emily Dickinson. They'll find all my poems in a closet when I'm dead and rotting. Then everyone will realize what they missed." Nikki slammed her fist down on the coffee table, knocking over the ashtray.

Kerri stared at her. Although she knew very little about poetry, she had read some of Nikki's work and had listened to her at the open mics. It didn't surprise her that Nikki was unpublished.

"I have a poem that I need to read to you guys. It's about a time I gave Pete a blowjob while we were driving down I-93 during a snowstorm. It's in my car. Hang on. I'll go get it. When I come back, Ryan, you can fuck me," Nikki said.

Ryan snapped to attention.

Nikki got up from the couch and zigzagged across the apartment, knocking against the walls and finally landing face down on Kerri's bed with her arms and legs sprawled out on the mattress.

She lifted her head. "But first I'm gonna take a little nap," she said. Her head fell like a sack of rocks on Kerri's pillow.

Ryan looked at Kerri. They both laughed. Kerri reached for the bottle on the coffee table and refilled her glass. She looked up at the canvas to avoid Ryan's gaze. The colors appeared then quickly disappeared as Ryan's voice snapped them like a thin branch.

"So. What's the deal with you, Kerri?" Ryan smiled and raised his eyebrows. The Dead had gone into a long version of "Dark Star". Pretending to be lost in the music, Kerri tapped the side of her wine glass with her index finger.

"Kerri?"

"I'm sorry. What?"

"What's the deal?" Ryan smiled. "Do you have a boyfriend?"

Kerri laughed. "You must be an accountant," she said.

"An accountant!" Ryan said, feigning offense. "Hell no! I'm a market analyst."

"Oh. My apologies," Kerri said, rolling her eyes.

"You never answered my question."

"What question?"

"Do you have a boyfriend?"

Kerri shook her head slowly and sighed. Unless her boyfriend was one of Ryan's close friends, it wouldn't make a difference. The order of his responses was predictable, transparent to the point of humor. Much like Ryan. If she said she had a boyfriend, he'd follow with the standard line of questions: How long have you been together? What does he do? After milking as much topical information as possible, he'd close with the clincher: Why isn't he here now? Which, of course, would imply that he, Ryan, would never leave her alone by herself; he'd attend to her every need. This was meant show Kerri what a great, caring and sensitive guy he was before he tried to stick his hand down her pants. He was a businessman. He dropped ten dollar bills and his phone number in tip jars; he danced after six drinks thinking that grinding his hips against a girl would turn her on and get him closer to the jackpot; he was every man that ever made a shameless attempt to come on to Kerri. He had a different name and a different cock he wanted to stick in her, but he was essentially the same man. He saw her in terms of availability, like real estate. He lacked color.

"No," Kerri said, "I just broke up with someone." She rubbed the shirt. Felt nothing.

"That's too bad. A pretty girl like you without someone to keep you company. I know what it's like. It can get pretty miserable being alone, eh?" Ryan said, refilling his glass. "I'm sure you have a lot of men interested in you. What's the problem?"

Kerri turned and looked at the canvas. What was the problem? Why couldn't she catch the picture, stop it there and paint it? Why did she always ruin things with her brush? Why couldn't she catch one man who didn't see her as beautiful? Someone who wanted an artist? Some men came close, like some of her pictures and paintings came close. But they always failed in the moments before completion—the final brushstrokes. James had no thrust; and Stephen lisped when he said his name; Mike picked his nose; and Plato never had any idea what the fuck he was talking about. Like the pictures, they were ruined when she interacted with them. Like the half-finished paintings that hung in a few small galleries and on the walls of her apartment, the half-men were marred by their imperfections.

Kerri stood up and slowly walked toward Ryan, her fingers unbuttoning the shirt as she approached. He looked at her and flushed with lust as he tried to lock his shit-eating grin behind gritted teeth. Her shirt opened and dropped to the floor.

He looked at the purple nipples. His jaw slackened. Kerri straddled his lap and locked her hands behind his head. She kissed his neck and felt his erection poke at her inner thigh from inside his jeans. She pressed her lips gently against his ear and nibbled on the lobe, blowing whispers. She could feel his pulse racing as his hands cupped her breasts. Her warm wine breath tickled his mouth as she pressed her lips roughly against his, kissing him and easing her tongue into his mouth. She pulled back and again kissed his neck, leaving a soft trail that stopped just below his ear.

"Ryan?" she whispered.

"Yeah…yeah?"

"Get the fuck out of here before I call the fucking cops."

She jumped off his lap and stood over him with her hands on her hips.

"What?"

She pointed to the door. He stood up, uncomfortably trying to hide his erection by pulling down his sweater. He swallowed the rest of his glass of wine. He started to say something. Kerri pointed to the door. He glaned at Nikki still passed out on the bed and left without another word.

Kerri sat down just as the door slammed. She looked up at the canvas. No picture. She had to be at the café at ten the next morning. Her boss liked her to show up half an hour early. She knew she would.

NOR'EASTER

Russ sat alone in the laundromat. The sound of the one active dryer—clunk clunk clink clunk—was rhythmic, soothing. He tapped his foot on the cracked cement floor and stared catatonically into the dryer's circular window. A pair of his blue flannel boxer shorts tumbled counter-clockwise to the top of the machine then dropped to the bottom. And began the cycle again.

Outside, the streets of Ashland, New Hampshire were vacant, with the exception of a group of townies loitering outside the Cumberland Farms across the road from the laundromat. They reached into the pockets of their battered denim jackets and pulled out cigarettes. Their deft movements seemed to disturb the tranquility, the calm before the snow.

Down both sides of Route 3 were dilapidated houses, old brick buildings containing small shops, hardware stores, and numerous picture windows filled with cobwebs and empty cardboard boxes. A half-mile south of Route 3, alongside the Squam River, stood the remnants of run-down mills and factories, where over the years the small town had taken futile stabs at various industries—lumber, hosiery, paper. As the twentieth century wore on, the logging moved north and new technology left the factories desolate. Ashland gradually became populated by a thin gene pool of gruff survivors; an incestuous breed of locals that remained more out of an inability to leave than a desire to stay. They roamed the barren streets in the forms of generations unchanged—embittered and oblivious, ugly and beaten.

Tired of watching his laundry, he walked outside for a cigarette. He waved his hand slowly through the cold air. It was something he'd picked up from the locals, who claimed they could stand outside, inhale deeply, look up at the sky, slowly move their hands through the air and tell whether or not it was going to snow. After five winters near the White Mountains, Russ found himself doing the same thing.

"We're going to get killed," he said to himself. He reached in his shirt pocket and grabbed a cigarette.

He was standing in front of the building, smoking and waving his hand in front of him, when a woman turned the corner. She was carrying a large wicker basket filled with clothes. On top of the stack she balanced a container of detergent, holding it steady with her chin. She was young. Under thirty. Her brown hair was pulled back into a bun, held in place by a pen. She wore a light blue sweatshirt and loose navy blue sweatpants. Her high cheekbones sloped gracefully into thin red lips. They cracked at the corners into a shy smile as she walked toward him. Her large blue eyes scanned him quickly, stopping at his own eyes.

He smiled back crookedly with his cigarette lodged between his lips and opened the door for her.

"Thank you," she said.

"No problem."

He leaned against the wall of the building and pulled another cigarette out of his pocket. He lit it with the old one and slumped his shoulders, resting one foot against the bricks in a leisurely James Dean pose. He resisted the urge to turn around and look at the girl while she loaded her laundry into the washing machines. He may have sensed something in their exchange of smiles, something raw and physical, but it'd been so long since a woman had smiled at him that his senses seemed unreliable. He pushed his short brown hair back with his hand and tossed the half-smoked cigarette on the sidewalk.

Back inside, he sat down in front of the dryer and resumed watching the blue boxer shorts.

"We're supposed to get snow tonight," the girl said. She was looking down, pouring detergent into the cap.

"Yeah, we're going to get killed," he said. He started to wave his hand in front of his face. But stopped.

"Oh yeah? How do you know?"

He shifted uncomfortably in his plastic seat.

"I heard it on the radio."

"Yeah, I heard the same thing." The girl closed the lid on the washing machine, inserted quarters and started the wash.

"You're not from around here, are you?" Russ asked. He hoped it sounded casual, not like a come-on.

"No. I'm from Jersey."

"Yeah. Me too. I mean, I'm not from Jersey. I'm just not from here. You know? New Hampshire? I'm originally from Boston. Well, not exactly the city. But around Boston."

The girl smiled.

Russ looked down at the floor. A pair of white panties had dropped from her basket. She hadn't noticed. He stared at them crumpled on the cracked cement and felt the beginnings of an erection poke against his inner thigh. He hunched over and rested his elbows on his knees to hide it.

The girl bent down to reach for her laundry basket and saw the panties. She blushed. Without looking at him she snatched them from the floor, opened the lid and dropped them in the washing machine. Then she looked at him and caught him staring. He immediately turned away and watched his spinning laundry again.

His erection reached full girth. He tried thinking of something other than her white panties. "It's definitely going to snow," he said, more to himself than the girl.

"What did you say?"

"I just said it was going to snow," he said without turning from the machine.

The dryer stopped. The blood drained from his face. His jaw dropped. Of all the times for the fucking dryer to stop? To have to stand up?

"I'm sorry. I thought you said something else," the girl said, smiling.

Russ turned and looked at her, secretly hoping she'd drop something else so he could jump up and stuff another quarter in the machine before she noticed anything. Realizing that wasn't going to happen, he decided on another approach.

He extended his hand from the sitting position. "I'm Russ by the way." He cringed at the sound of his own name. He tried not to think about being Russ. Most of the time, living alone, he pretended he didn't have a name. There was nothing. He liked being nothing. It was all right. But now, with his hand extended, he was RUSS. Worse yet, he was Russ with an adolescent hard-on.

"I'm Melanie. Good to meet you, Russ," she said, walking over to him, shaking his hand.

Russ covered his crotch with his left arm. "Do you live in Ashland?" he asked.

"Yeah. Do you?"

"Yeah. Well, technically I live in New Hampton on Lake Winona, about five miles down the road. But I used to live in Plymouth. Went to school there. Graduated last year," he said. He stopped himself before he went on. The thought of himself and the pitiful state of his life made his erection subside.

"Oh, really? I used to go to Plymouth, too."

"When?"

She thought a moment. "About six years ago. I was only there for a year though."

"Oh, that must've been the year before I started."

"Really. So, what are you doing now?"

Russ turned and looked out the window of the laundromat. He thought about lying, but knew he didn't have it in him. "I'm a cook," he said.

"Oh, really? I wait tables."

"Where at?" he asked.

"The Snowy Owl. Have you heard of it?"

"Yeah, actually I have. In fact, I think I know someone who works there, or at least used to work there. I worked with him in Waterville a while back. Nick Quinn?"

Melanie's eyes widened. Her mouth dropped slightly. Then she smoothed it into an uneasy smile. "I know Nick. I used to date him for awhile," she said, pursing her lips.

"Oh, I'm sorry. Is that a sore subject?" Russ' entire body cringed. Fuck, he thought.

"No. I like Nick. He left there a couple of months ago. Moved to Florida. Had enough of New Hampshire. Can't really blame him," Melanie said, sitting down next to Russ in a plastic chair.

They sat together, listening to the washing machines.

"Are you going to take your clothes out of the dryer? It finished a while ago," Melanie said.

"Oh, shit. I didn't even notice it stopped." Russ stood up and walked to the machine with his basket. As he was unloading his laundry, he glanced out the window. "It's starting," he said.

Melanie turned and watched the first flakes of the storm flutter down.

"I should get going before the roads get too bad," Russ said.

"Yeah, it might get bad pretty quick."

Russ placed his basket on the chair and dug in his pockets for his car keys.

"It was nice meeting you," he said.

"Yes. Definitely. Nice meeting you. Drive safe," Melanie said.

He started to leave, then stopped.

"Uh, what are you doing later?" he asked.

"Well, we're supposed to get—"

"I mean, if the roads aren't that bad, would you want to meet for a drink or something?" He looked at her standing in front of him, her dark hair lightened by the halogen bulbs on the ceiling.

She smiled nervously, rubbing the back of her neck. "Sure. I mean, don't kill yourself if the roads are bad or anything."

"No, no, no…I won't. Besides, when I was outside earlier, it didn't really feel like it was going to snow that hard," he said.

"Didn't you say we were supposed to killed?"

"No. I said I heard it on the weather forecast. But you know… um, the old saying: if you don't like the weather in New England, wait an hour."

"Yeah," she said, laughing. "Okay. Where do you want to go?"

"I assume you know where the Broken Wheel is?"

Melanie laughed dryly. "It's the only nice bar in Ashland."

"Around 7:00?"

"Yeah, I can do that. It gives me enough time to go home, shower and put on some clean clothes," Melanie said.

They laughed uncomfortably.

"Clean clothes," Russ said, looking down at the basket under his arm.

"But don't worry about it if the roads are too bad. I mean, I don't want you to kill yourself," Melanie said.

"Well, why don't you give me your number, and if I can't make it I'll call you and let you know."

"Sure," Melanie said, pulling the pen from her hair. Russ tore the top off his pack of cigarettes, flattened it out and handed it to her. She wrote down her phone number and handed it to him. He put it in his pocket.

He ran his hand through his hair and sighed. "Well, hopefully I'll see you tonight," he said.

"Yeah. It was nice meeting you, Russ," she said.

Russ cringed. *Russ*. "Very nice meeting you, too," he said. He turned and walked out the door into the empty street.

A thin sprinkling of snow had accumulated on the rooftops and sidewalks, giving Ashland the picturesque, postcard visage of small town New Hampshire. Across the road the townies stood in front of Cumberland Farms smoking cigarettes and holding Budweiser tall boys in gloved hands.

Russ stood outside his car, which was parked in front of the laundromat. He held his basket and watched the townies. They were smiling. They were cement fixtures in front of the store, blemishes on the postcard. They sweated at work, went home to overweight wives chain-smoking menthols and mangy kids with Spaghetti-O stains on their fingers and lips, and generations of hapless ghosts moaning through the pain of backs broken over and over again. They were also postcards, the ones no one bought. The real New Hampshire.

Russ stepped inside his car, placing the laundry basket on the passenger seat. He drove away, glancing quickly inside the laundromat. The snow started to thicken on his windshield. The wipers worked furiously to push it aside.

Russ placed the bowl of Cheerios on the coffee table and dug his hand between the cushions of the couch, searching for the remote control. He pulled out two nickels, a penny and a pinch of lint. He kneeled down on the floor, peeking underneath the couch. He found the remote next to an empty can of Bud Light and turned on the television and VCR, glancing up at a clock hanging on the wall. It was 5:15. He placed the bowl on his lap and scooped spoonfuls of Cheerios into his mouth as the movie rewound.

He turned his head and glanced out the front window of his cottage. The snow came down hard. He watched a white birch tree sway in a breeze coming off the lake. The wind shook the snow off the thin branches. He knew they would be covered again within minutes.

He didn't wait for the movie to finish rewinding. He hit Play and settled back into the couch. On the screen, a busty blonde in a tight police officer's uniform slapped a billy club against her palm. A prisoner—a thin man with a closely trimmed goatee and blond hair greased back with Vaseline—picked at his teeth with a toothpick, watching her with a slick grin.

"The warden said you have been bad. Very bad," the blonde said, reaching her hand between the bars and gently patting his cheek.

"It seems I'm always getting into something," the prisoner said, mumbling his words while chewing the toothpick.

"It's time to inspect you for any concealed weapons," she said, reaching into his pants. "Ooh. Here's a big gun. Who were you planning on shooting it at?" The music, which sounded like it'd been made with a Casio keyboard, kicked in.

Russ placed the bowl of Cheerios on the table and, without taking his eyes off the screen, sat on his right hand. He'd memorized the scene. The blonde would get down on her knees and look up at the prisoner while stroking his unusually large cock, telling him how she'd need to inspect it further, to see if it was loaded. The prisoner would smile and tell her that it's fine with him and spit out the toothpick. Russ wasn't one of those guys who fast-forwarded through the dialogue for the sex scenes. He watched the movies straight through, letting the anticipation build as his own weight slowly cut off the circulation to his right hand. He thought of meeting Melanie at the bar later that night. He envisioned the simplistic and terse conversation of *Jailhouse Cock*, as the evening's events slipped naturally and effortlessly into sex.

"Now it's my turn to inspect you."

Russ slid his left hand down his pants and stroked himself until he was sure his right hand was completely numb. When it was, he'd quickly switch hands—a technique he'd picked up from a guy he'd lived with in the dorms. When the hand was numb and no longer part of him, it took on the various anatomical parts of an actual woman. His hand became a warm, soothing tongue and soft lips or a damp pussy or simply a female hand feverishly stroking him toward climax. He could smell the woman on the television screen, feel her hot breath on the back of his neck. His erection throbbed.

"I love your cock in my pussy. Now put it in my ass. Come on, you stupid fuck, put it in my ass!"

"Oh yeah...I'm gonna put it in your ass," the prisoner whispered.

Russ switched hands. He watched her blood red lips, pursed in the form of a kiss and her large silicone breasts shake under the tremor of each thrust from the prisoner, as he stood behind her, violently smacking her ass cheeks. He pictured Melanie and himself in a prison cell and the white panties crumpled and loose around one of her ankles. He bit down on his bottom lip.

"Oh, oh, oh! Yeah. Come on my ass! I want you to come on my ass!"

Russ felt his legs weaken. His pulse fluttered and his body stiffened. He pulled his T-shirt up with his left hand, closed his eyes and ejaculated onto his bare stomach.

He lay still as the circulation returned to his hand and looked out at the white birch—thin and alone. He reached under the couch for an old T-shirt he kept there specifically for this purpose. He wiped himself clean and stopped the tape just as the prisoner pulled out of the blonde.

Russ listened to the wind outside. He wondered if the roads were drivable. He knew that he was going into town either way. He picked up the cordless phone on the coffee table and dialed the number on the lid of the cigarette box.

"Hello?"

"Melanie?"

"Yes."

"This is Russ." He cringed saying it.

"Oh. Hi Russ. What's up?"

Russ stared at the blank screen on the television, picked up the starched T-shirt beside him and tossed it across the room. "Oh, not much. Just watching a movie," he said.

"I'm assuming you're not going to make it. The reports are calling it a Nor'easter," Melanie said. Russ heard a child's voice in the background.

"Yeah, I'm coming anyway. I'll be fine. I have front-wheel drive. We'll only have a couple inches by then. Besides, I need to get out of this place for a bit."

"Are you sure? I don't want you to kill yourself trying to make it here. We could always do it some other time."

Russ looked around his cottage at the ripped wallpaper and the dishes stacked in the sink. "No. I'm coming tonight," he said. "I'll see you at 7:00. Right?"

"Okay. If you're sure. I'll see you then," Melanie said.

"See you then." Russ hung up the phone and glanced out the window. It was nearly pitch dark. The wind shook another layer of snow from the tree's frail branches.

Russ drove slowly through the swirling cloud of snow in the headlights. His knuckles were white against the steering wheel as he eased the vehicle through a sharp curve on the narrow Winona Road. He turned off the radio and listened to the strained hum of the engine. The wipers fought in vain to clear a line of vision for him. If he swerved off the left side of the road, he'd drop off a small precipice onto the ice of Lake Winona. He hugged the right side.

He reached for a cigarette from his pack on the dashboard, but as soon as his hand left the wheel, the car fishtailed. He caught the wheel and regained control of the vehicle. He took a deep breath, feeling his nerves twitch when a large, black form suddenly appeared in front of the car.

A pair of incandescent red eyes met Russ'. He stomped on the brake petal. The deer stood frozen in the dull gleam of the headlights before gracefully leaping into the dark mesh of woods, barely missing the front bumper. The car slid off the right side of the road and slammed sideways into a snowbank.

Russ stared ahead with his mouth open, gripping the steering wheel. He wiggled his toes and rolled his neck then slowly took his hands off the wheel, bending his arms and fingers. His heart palpitated. He leaned his head back and placed his hands on his chest. The engine had stopped. The wind whipped around the car, rattling the windows.

The wipers continued to toss the snow aside. After catching his breath, he turned the key and stepped on the accelerator. The engine coughed and clicked. Nothing. He flipped the headlights and windshield wipers off and tried again.

The engine coughed weakly and turned over. He threw it into reverse and stepped on the gas. The front wheels spun, then abruptly jerked the car back onto the road. He turned the wipers and headlights back on, put it in drive and continued on his way.

He drove past the lake and a straight stretch of pasture. He knew there would be streetlights less than a mile ahead. Where there were streetlights, there was the bar. In the bar, Melanie waited, maybe wearing white panties beneath a pair of clean pants. Her legs were warm; the panties were warm. His hands were cold. He wished he had brought a pair of gloves.

He tapped his cigarette into an empty can of Diet Coke. Then something occurred to him, which he hadn't considered in his haste to drive to town: What if she didn't show?

The Broken Wheel Tavern was an old two-story farmhouse, which two New York City businessmen bought and renovated in the mid-Eighties. Just off I-93, it thrived on tourists driving to and from the White Mountains. The building itself stuck out as a rare and beautiful oddity in an otherwise run-down town. The restaurant was decorated with an eighteenth century colonial motif: wooden barrels with butter churning paddles in the corners and farming relics buffed and polished with lacquer hanging on the walls. The inside smelled of oak and sandalwood incense.

The bottom floor was the dining area. A narrow stairwell wound upstairs from the dining room into the tavern. The tavern had a fireplace in the far corner and large cushiony couches set around it. The bar was against the back wall—a polished, solid oak structure with tall stools in front of it. Easy listening jazz trickled from the ceiling, a tranquil mixture of saxophones and soft bass lines.

On a stool in the center of the bar, with a pint of Bud Light in front of him, Russ sat alone. He watched the Boston Bruins on a muted television and sipped his beer. The bartender, a handsome man in his late twenties with soft features and a smooth face, kept his elbows on the bar as he leaned forward and stared blankly into the fireplace. He wore a denim collared shirt with the Broken Wheel's logo on the left front pocket. Another man, older, distinguished and well-dressed in khakis and blue fleece pulled over a dress shirt, sat in the corner of the bar. He was scribbling in a notepad with a drink in front of him.

Russ reached in the pocket of his newly washed jeans and placed his cigarettes on the bar. He pulled one from his pack and lit it. The tap on his shoulder startled him.

"I'm sorry I'm late. I had to wait for the babysitter to show up," Melanie said. "Honestly, I didn't think you'd make it." Her brown hair, sprinkled with snowflakes, fell almost to her shoulders. She had applied lipstick. Her cheeks were blushed from the cold. She removed her coat and sat down on the stool next to him. She wore a tight blue sweater and black slacks that hugged her hips and thighs. Her figure was full, yet firm. Womanly. Russ turned on his stool to face her.

"I'm really glad you made it," he said, staring at her forehead to keep his eyes from looking at her chest.

"What can I get you, Melanie?" the bartender asked. He smiled and winked at her.

"I'll have a whiskey sour," Melanie said, folding her hands on the bar. "By the way, Kevin, this my friend, Russ. Russ, Kevin."

The bartender reached over the bar and shook Russ' hand. "Good to meet you," Kevin said.

"Nice meeting you," Russ said, smiling politely.

"You said a whiskey sour, right?" Kevin asked, reaching down for the sour mix.

Melanie nodded and brushed a few remaining snowflakes from her hair.

"Did you say you had to get a babysitter? You have a kid?" Russ asked, recalling the voice in the background when they'd spoken on the phone earlier.

Melanie smiled. "Yeah, a son. Robbie. He'll be five in August."

"I would've never guessed. I mean, you don't look like a mother," Russ said and wanted to slap himself in the forehead.

"It was just one of those things, you know. I was young and irresponsible."

"Is the father around? If you don't mind me getting too personal."

"It's all right. No," Melanie said. "His father lives in Ohio. I never hear from him."

Kevin put the drink in front of Melanie. "I'm surprised you're out tonight," he said, smiling at her.

"Yeah. I figured I wouldn't have to wait for drinks," Melanie said.

"Not while I'm working," Kevin said, putting a coaster underneath her drink.

"By the way, where did you park?" Melanie asked, putting her hand on Russ' forearm.

"I'm in that lot across the street. Why? Are they going to tow me?"

"No, but you're going to get plowed in if you plan on staying the night," Kevin said.

"No. I think I'll try to drive home," Russ said.

"Don't be ridiculous. You can stay on my couch. We'll worry about it tomorrow," Melanie said, sipping her drink. She placed it back on the bar with a streak of lipstick smeared on the edge of the glass.

"Okay," Russ said, smiling uncomfortably and reaching for his beer. He looked at Melanie while she watched the hockey game on the television. She didn't look like a mother. She turned and caught Russ examining her face. The two exchanged quick smiles, and shyly turned their attention to the television.

"I almost hit a deer on the way here," Russ said, snapping the silence. "The son of a bitch jumped right in front of my car."

"Oh my God!" Melanie said, placing her hand over her mouth. The man at the other end of the bar looked up from his notebook.

"It put a good scare in me," Russ said.

"I bet. A girl I used to work with," Melanie said, placing her hand on top of Russ', "her boyfriend was the first to arrive on the scene of a moose accident last year. You should have heard him describe it. Apparently, it completely scalped the driver. Like pulling off a mask. It really messed him up seeing it. His girlfriend said he just sat in their room and smoked cigarettes after that."

"Yeah, a lot of weird shit happens around here," Kevin said, grabbing a rag from a bucket and wiping down some glasses. "Hey, Melanie, can you watch the bar? I have to take a leak."

"Sure," Melanie said. The old man at the end of the bar lifted his head, looked around and buried it back into his notebook.

Russ lit a cigarette and inadvertently exhaled in Melanie's face.

"I'm sorry," he said, reaching out and trying to pull back the smoke. He lifted his hand and ran it through her hair, holding the smoke in his fingertips.

Melanie turned and smiled. "No, it's okay. I used to smoke before...well, you know. Before I had Robbie."

"I still didn't mean to blow smoke in your face," he said. He kept his hand in her hair, his fingers lightly massaging her scalp. She lifted her hand and touched his cheek. Then she turned to watch the snow falling outside the windows.

Russ removed his hand. "I'm sorry about that," he said.

"No. Don't be." They looked at each other again.

"Now it's my turn to ask a personal question," she said. "How'd you get that scar on your head?"

"It's a long story. You really don't want to hear it. Trust me."

"I do," she said, and smiled at him.

"So what's the deal with the bartender? How do you know him?" Russ asked.

"I used to come here a lot. I probably shouldn't tell you this, but he used to be a teacher down in Concord. I think he taught English, or maybe it was History, that's not important.

"Anyway," Melanie leaned closer to Russ, watching the bathroom door, "he slept with one of his students—a sixteen year old girl. The girl's parents found a note she wrote to him and hit the roof. He was forced to resign. The schoolboard told him to pack his stuff and get out of Concord. He left and moved up here where he figured nobody would find out. He's been bartending here since. Well, that's what he does for a living. His real job, from what I can gather, is trying to get in my pants."

"Shit, that's crazy. What a scumbag!"

"He's not that bad of a guy. He told me the story one night when he was drunk here. He said something about his girlfriend leaving him, and he was rebounding."

"With a sixteen year old girl?"

"Yeah, I know. I guess the parents never went through with the charges. The girl wouldn't testify. He got lucky," Melanie said, as the bathroom door swung open. Kevin walked out, shaking his hands dry.

"You sure it's not a problem that I stay on your couch?" Russ asked.

"No, not at all. As long as you don't mind my son waking you up. He's usually up around 7:00 in the morning for his cartoons," Melanie said.

Kevin walked back behind the bar and grabbed Russ' empty mug. "All right, I got a joke for you. I heard it from a guy who was in here the other night."

"Okay," Melanie said.

"Why can't you get a blowjob in Massachusetts on weekends?" Kevin said, pouring a Bud Light from the tap into the mug.

Melanie glanced at Russ. "I don't know," she said.

"Because all the cocksuckers are up here." Kevin smiled, placed the beer in front of Russ and waited for a response. Russ shook his head and smirked. Melanie sighed.

"In the restaurant industry, those 'cocksuckers' pay our bills," Melanie said, handing her empty glass to Kevin.

"It's a joke," he said, dejectedly grabbing the Dewar's from the shelf behind him. He turned and looked at the old man, who had lifted his head from his notebook. He was laughing, tapping his empty glass with his index finger.

"The cocksuckers are all here. I should write that down," he said.

Kevin raised his eyebrows and nodded his head at Russ and Melanie. "See. *Someone* has a sense of humor." Kevin turned to the old man. "Another Dewar's, sir?"

The man nodded, wiping his eyes with his sleeve.

Outside the snow continued to accumulate. The mills and old buildings assumed a new, pristine white form.

In the tavern tongues and spirits loosened. The old man, Don, a retired college professor from Keene, put aside his notebook and joined the conversation, his cheeks flushed from the scotch. Underneath the bar, Russ held Melanie's hand.

Kevin settled the tabs and formally shut down the bar at 11:00 p.m., two hours before last call. He told the shift manager he'd close up, and the restaurant, which had been empty since 8:00, was silent with the exception of voices and jazz emanating from the tavern.

Kevin poured the last round for free and joined the others for a beer. He sat on a stool and lit a cigarette.

"So what did you teach, Don?" Russ asked, lifting his glass to Kevin in acknowledgement of the free drink.

"A little of this and that. Mostly British Literature and writing."

Kevin rubbed his chin and turned to Don, squinting like he was reading the wrinkles on his face.

"So you're a writer, I take it," Russ said, giving Melanie's hand a squeeze.

"Jesus, you look familiar," Kevin said to Don. "I know I've seen you somewhere before. Have you been in here?"

"Yes, but it was quite some time ago. It was around ten years ago when I did a presentation at Plymouth State."

"My alma mater," Russ said, looking down at his hand holding Melanie's. It looked like a cook's hand—calloused and burned in spots.

Suddenly, Kevin's eyes widened. He mashed his cigarette out in the ashtray. "Fuck me. I know where I've seen you. You're Donald Silverman. The poet. You won a goddamn Pulitzer."

The old man winced and reached for his drink.

"I used to teach English. I'm a big fan of your work," Kevin said. He reached over the bar for a scrap of paper by the register. "Could I get your autograph? Oh man, I love *The Ground Below Zero*. I have it on my nightstand right now."

"I really wish you wouldn't ask. It makes me feel uncomfortable," Don said, holding up his palm and turning his head.

Russ looked at Kevin. "Just leave the guy alone. We're having a good time. Let's not make a big production of this."

"Do *you* know who this man is? He's a contemporary legend. I just want a damn autograph." Kevin's voice rose. He scowled at Russ.

Don stood up and grabbed his coat from the stool next to him. He picked up his notebook and placed his pen in his shirt pocket. "I really should be going. Thank you. It was nice meeting everyone."

"You know, I read somewhere that you were an asshole," Kevin said, crumpling the scrap paper and throwing it at Don.

"Lay off, will you?" Russ said, letting Melanie's hand slip from his own. He turned toward Kevin. Kevin stared back and scoffed.

Don shook his head and put on his coat. "You know what, Kevin? You were right. All the cocksuckers *are* up here, only I wouldn't say exclusively on weekends." He waved to Russ and Melanie and passed quietly down the spiral staircase and out the front door.

Kevin said nothing, clenching his fists and staring at Russ.

"So you're taking this little bitch home with you tonight, Melanie? I don't think you have anything to worry about. He'll stay on the couch."

Russ smiled at Kevin. His heart raced and his forehead started to sweat as he digested the comment. Kevin's eyes went cold as he stared him down. Russ turned to Melanie.

She shook her head. "Not everyone can find little teenage girls to play with," she said, standing up from the stool and putting on her coat.

"Fuck both of you," Kevin said. "Get the fuck out of here!"

"Thanks, barkeep. It was a pleasure," Russ said, standing up. His knees were trembling. He waved at Kevin.

"We'll think of you tonight," Melanie said over her shoulder as she and Russ walked down the stairs. Russ put his arm around Melanie. They stood in front of the door.

"You're incredible," he said, running his hand through her hair and kissing her on the lips. Her mouth was warm and smooth; her tongue had the slight taste of whiskey. She's real, breathing and kissing me, Russ thought.

They opened the front door and walked, hand in hand, into the fresh snowfall; into the streets of the new town of Ashland.

They walked three-quarters of a mile to Melanie's place. It was a trailer mounted on cinderblocks about fifty yards from the Squam River.

"Here we are," Melanie said, kicking the snow off the steps leading to the door. The flashing blue and white lights of a television shone from inside.

"If I didn't have a buzz, I'd be freezing my ass off," Russ said, stuffing his hands in his pockets and jumping up and down. He wished he'd brought his gloves.

Melanie opened the door, and Russ followed her inside. They walked into the dark kitchen and removed their boots. Their toes were cold, damp and sticking to their wet socks. Russ took off his socks, rubbed his wet feet and listened to David Letterman deliver his opening monologue from the other room. Melanie turned on the kitchen light.

The kitchen was small. It had the essentials: a sink with dirty dishes stacked neatly inside, wooden cabinets with chipped white paint, an old gas oven, a small microwave and toaster on the linoleum counter, and an old oak kitchen table with two sturdy wooden chairs around it. A window by the sink overlooked the river—unfrozen and violently flowing, swallowing the snow.

"Tiffany, I'm back," Melanie said as Russ followed her through a narrow doorway into the other room.

On a couch, a young girl slept with the remote control in her hand. The living room was also small, yet tidy and comfortable. A coffee table sat in front of the couch with a stack of unopened bills, a candle and two coloring books on top of it. The television was propped up on a small wooden stand, pushed against the wall under the window.

Melanie leaned over the couch and nudged the sleeping girl— a chubby teenager with short, blond hair and a face speckled with acne.

The girl opened her eyes and looked drowsily up at Melanie. "Oh. Hi, Mel," she said, sitting up and stretching her thick arms. "What time is it?"

"It's around 11:30. Sorry I'm late," Melanie said. "Did Robbie give you any trouble?"

"No, none at all. He went to bed around 8:00. I let him watch his Power Rangers video, and he went to sleep right after that," Tiffany said, looking at Russ, who was standing behind Melanie with his arms crossed, rocking back on his heels.

"Oh, I'm sorry. Tiffany, this is Russ. Russ, Tiffany. My babysitter." Russ and Tiffany waved to each other. Melanie walked down a narrow hallway and peeked inside the first door on her left. "Sound asleep," she said.

"I think the Power Rangers did him in," Tiffany said, reaching for her purse on the floor.

"You can sleep here if you'd like. Russ can take the floor in my room," Melanie said, nudging him in the ribs.

"No. It's just a little snow. I can make it." Tiffany stood up and grabbed her coat off the back of the couch.

"Are you sure?"

"Yeah, I'm sure," she said.

"Be sure to give a quick call when you get in. Just I so I know you're safe."

Tiffany followed Melanie into the kitchen.

"It was nice meeting you," Tiffany said, lifting her hand shyly as she left the room.

"Yeah, same here," Russ said.

He walked down the hallway and peeked inside the first door on his right—the bathroom. His bladder was heavy from the beer. He felt along the wall until he found the light switch. The room, like the rest of the house, was small and cloistered. The shower curtain matched the rug, and the sink and tub were scrubbed meticulously. Russ thought of his own bathroom where different forms of mold and fungus grew in separate areas of the tub and hair, congealed toothpaste and shaving cream lined the sink. He pissed into the clean toilet. He washed his hands and walked back into the living room.

Melanie was lounging on the couch with her feet on the coffee table. "I see you found the bathroom," she said.

"Yeah, it's always interesting to see how differently women live."

"I'm sorry. The place is a pigsty. I wasn't really expecting to have a guest tonight."

"This is a mess?" Russ asked, laughing.

"Yeah, look at it," Melanie said, patting the cushion next to her on the couch. "Anyway, have a seat. I'd offer you a beer, but I don't have any in the fridge. Do you want something else to drink?"

"No. I'm fine," Russ said and sat down beside her. His head was light and clouded.

They stared at the television. Russ rubbed the back of his neck as Melanie pursed her lips and made soft clicking noises with her tongue.

"Do you like Letterman?" she asked as she snuggled up to him, resting her head on his shoulder. With her long hair inches from his nose, he could smell the subtle scent of strawberries from her shampoo.

"Yeah, Leno annoys me," Russ said, putting his arm around her back and laughing, uncomfortably, at one of Letterman's goofy faces at the camera.

"Me too."

"I can't stand his chin. And his laugh annoys the hell out of me," Russ said.

"Yeah."

Russ looked at Melanie's head resting on his shoulder. Her brown hair looked blue in the television light. She breathed slowly. There was a heartbeat and blood rushing through her veins. She was real, alive—not a buxom prison guard with mounds of red lipstick to smear on his face with one open-mouthed kiss. He rubbed her scalp with his fingers, as if to confirm her presence next to him.

"My old roommate, Susan, and I used to watch Letterman all the time in the dorms," Melanie said, more to herself than Russ. "We'd come home from some frat party on Thursday or Friday night, order Chinese food and watch Letterman sitting in the lounge of our dorm. All the drunk guys would stumble in around 1:00 and always try to pick us up. Susan was gorgeous. I was always so jealous of her. Beautiful blond hair. Fantastic body."

"Do you still talk to her?"

"Nah, that spring I got pregnant and had to drop out after the semester," Melanie said. "I've talked to her a couple of times since. Last I knew she was going to graduate and become an elementary school teacher. But we haven't talked in years. It's weird how that happens. She was the last *real* female friend I've had. Since Robbie was born, I just don't…you know, have a lot of time. Or friends."

He placed his hand gently on her cheek.

"I mean, don't listen to me. I'm just feeling those whiskey sours. I'm sorry."

"No, it's okay."

The wind rattled the windows. He looked at her and held her chin in his hand, waiting for her to make the first slight movement. She lifted her head from his shoulder and gently kissed his neck, then his mouth. He loosened his jaw as her lips gently pressed against his own. He ran his hand through her hair, and tentatively touched her stomach with the other. Slowly he moved toward her breast. She rubbed his inner thigh. His breathing quickened. She gently ran her hand over the swell of the erection in his jeans. He kissed her harder and slid his hand under her tight sweater, then under her bra. He felt the warm flesh of her breast. Her nipple hardened between his fingers.

"Do you want to go to my bedroom?" she whispered.

He nodded, drying his lips with the back of his hand.

She led him down the narrow hallway into the bedroom next to the boy's. She switched on the light. The bed was in the far corner with a small nightstand beside it. Her laundry basket sat in the center of the room; the clothes folded and still unpacked. He thought again of her white panties. He wondered if she was wearing them. He stared at himself in a mirror mounted to the wall, his thin frame and the awkward hard-on sticking out in his jeans.

"Can I turn off the light?" he said. "I'm a little self-conscious."

"Sure," she said, sitting down on the bed. He switched off the light and sat down next to her. She kissed his ear and fell back onto the bed, pulling him on top of her. He tugged at the hem of her sweater. She raised her arms. He slipped it off her and tossed it on the bedroom floor. He fidgeted with her bra, until she unfastened it for him with one quick snap of her fingers. He took both breasts in his hands and squeezed them.

"Easy. Be gentle," she whispered.

"Sorry," he said, blushing in the dark.

They turned onto their sides, facing each other. She unbuttoned his jeans, reached for his zipper then wiggled them down to his thighs. He took off his shirt and tossed it next to her sweater. She slipped her hand into his boxer shorts and started gently stroking him.

He groaned. He tried to stop himself; he hated the way it sounded. But with each stroke, another groan escaped from him. He unfastened the top button of her pants and slowly pulled them off her hips, letting her legs slide out one at a time. He ran his hand over the moist crotch of her panties. He could tell in the dim light that came through the window that they weren't white. He slid his hand down and eased his finger into her. She moaned. He pulled down her panties and massaged her with his index finger. Her hips made slow circles as she adjusted his hand, showing him the spot.

"That feels so good," she said.

She let him rub her like that for a while. He kissed her lips and breasts as he did it. Then she sat up.

"Why don't you take those off," she said. He pulled off his underwear and threw them onto the floor, then lay down.

She took him into her mouth slowly. He bit down on his bottom lip, holding back a loud moan. She continued, using her hands and mouth in tandem. He felt an orgasm beginning to build. He was afraid to come. It was too soon. Way too soon. He grabbed her head with his hands, stopping her.

"Your turn," he said, laying her on her back. He kissed her neck, then moved down to her breasts and licked slow circles around her nipples, biting each one gently before moving down to her stomach. He stopped there, kissing her bellybutton, licking her hips and thighs. And stopped again. It had been such a long time since he'd gone down on a woman. He hesitated for a moment, then slowly worked his way in. He licked her timidly at first. She tasted good. He moved his tongue gently around until he found the tiny button. He held down her hips with his hands. She moaned loudly. He continued until he felt her thighs tighten around his head as she came.

Afterwards, he lay down next to her and kissed her neck.

"That was really great," she said.

She reached into the drawer of the nightstand, pulled out a condom and tore off the corner of the packet with her teeth. She rolled it onto him, then straddled his hips.

"I'm not always this easy, you know," she said in a sultry voice. "It's just that I really like you."

The comment stunned him. He lay frozen on his back as she guided him into her with her hand. She moaned. She was wet and warm and slippery and fucking him. And she *liked* him. Her hips undulated, taking him deep inside of her, gaining intensity.

"Ooh…yeah. Oh, Russ."

He again hated the sound of his name, especially from her lips in the middle of sex. He didn't want to be Russ the cook, or Russ the pervert, or Russ the boyfriend, much less Russ the stepfather. He looked at the laundry basket again. In the distance, beyond Melanie's moans, he could hear plows scraping the pavement. His entire body relaxed. His arms fell by his side.

Melanie stopped.

"Russ, are you okay?" she asked. He slid out of her.

"The plows are out," he said.

"What?"

"I can hear the plow trucks."

The sound of the plows grew closer. They listened in silence. The telephone rang.

Russ woke from a restless sleep. The plows continued, but the sound seemed distant. Behind the shade, light cracked into the bedroom. He could hear the television in the other room. Melanie slept with her back turned to him. She had a pillow pulled over her head.

Russ climbed out of bed. He was naked. He found his underwear on the floor and put it on. Melanie lay wearing a T-shirt with a comforter pulled to her chest. His mouth was dry. He rubbed his temples. There was a slight throb in the side of his head. He lifted the comforter and looked at her body—the curve of her hip and her smooth white legs. He didn't have anything to say. He stood over the bed looking down at her, the pillow covering her head.

He quickly dressed and walked down the hallway into the living room. A young boy with brown curly hair sat cross-legged on the floor in front of the television, mesmerized by a cartoon. Sensing Russ, he turned around and looked up at him with large blue eyes the size of bottle caps. Melanie's eyes.

"Hi," the boy said.

"Hi." Russ looked down at the boy, lifting his palm.

"I'm Robbie. Who are you?"

"I'm Russ."

"What were you doing in Mommy's room?"

Russ attempted to swallow his spit, but his mouth was too dry.

"Well," he said, running his hand through his matted hair, "I'm a friend of your mother's, and…she wasn't feeling well last night, so I stayed to take care of her."

"Oh."

Robbie turned back to the television.

"Are you going to stay for breakfast?" he said over his shoulder.

"No, I can't stay for breakfast."

"Oh."

"I have to be somewhere in a little while," Russ said, looking away from the boy.

"Mommy makes good pancakes," the boy said with his back turned to Russ. Carnival-like music came from the television set.

An emptiness rumbled in Russ' stomach. It was painful. He knew if he stood there any longer, he'd stay for pancakes.

"I have to go now," Russ said.

"Oh."

He wished he'd taken the time to kiss Melanie before he left. He opened his palm and waved to Robbie, who continued staring at the television.

"Nice meeting you, Robbie."

"Bye."

He walked into the cold morning air. Everything was white with the exception of the sky—clear blue, bright and unbroken by clouds. The luminescence of the sunlight reflecting off the snow blinded him. He squinted and placed his hand as a visor over his eyes. A wicked gust of wind smacked the side of his face. He put his head down, pulled his coat over his nose and slowly walked the three-quarters of a mile to the parking lot where he'd left his car.

The trucks had plowed around his car, leaving nothing but an antenna sticking out of a pile of snow. He looked at the buried car and sighed. He turned around and began heading back in the direction of the Cumberland Farms to buy a shovel.

In front of the Cumberland Farms, two townies stood against the brick wall smoking cigarettes. Both were of an indeterminate age wearing ragged winter coats and tight blue jeans. They peered at Russ suspiciously as he approached.

"You park the Escort near the Broken Wheel?" asked the taller of the two men. He was unshaven and gaunt, with a dirt color to his complexion. He sucked on his cigarette.

Russ looked at him.

"Yeah."

"Worst storm we seen 'round heah in twelve yeahs. I was just tellin' Hank, I ain't seen one this bad since '78," the shorter man said. He was stocky. His bottom front teeth were missing and his lip curled over the gap. He wore an old, ragged New England Patriots snow cap with the emblem of the Patriot snapping a football hanging on by a few stitches.

"They say the kids ain't gonna be in school for a couple of days. I heard the power at the school's out," Hank said.

Russ nodded.

"Bet'cha you need a shovel," said the short man.

"Yeah," Russ said.

"I was gonna have you towed last night, but not even the tow trucks was willin' to go out in that shit. I plowed 'round it this morning. Don'tcha know there ain't no parkin' during storms?" Hank asked, wiping his nose with the sleeve of his coat.

"I was told my car would be all right in the parking lot."

The two men looked at each other and laughed—hoarse, smoky guffaws.

"There's ain't no parkin' anywhere durin' storms. You shoulda been towed, but it was too shitty to tow anyone," the shorter man said, tucking his cigarette in the gap between his bottom teeth and inhaling.

"Well, thanks for not towing me."

"I can get'cha outta there in no time. I'll plow ya out for forty bucks," Hank said, dropping his cigarette in the snow.

"That's all right. I'll just buy a shovel," Russ said.

"Good fuckin' luck," Hank said.

Both men looked at each other and laughed again.

"Your best bet's lettin' me plow ya out." Hank motioned toward a battered brown pickup truck with a plow attached to the front parked across the street in front of the laundromat. He stared at Russ with beady, black eyes squinting in the reflection off the snow.

"No, I'll just buy a shovel," Russ said.

"Suit yourself. Goddamn moron," Hank said. The shorter man, obviously pleased by Hank's remark, nudged his friend in the ribs.

Russ walked inside the store. The heat burned his cold face. He rubbed his palms together, letting his fingers absorb the warmth. An overweight woman in a ratty red sweatshirt with a brown bear on the front watched him from behind the counter. Long, greasy strands of knotted black hair extended the length of her back. Her face looked like a flat ball of dough with raisins for eyes. She sat on a stool with her arms folded.

Russ found a stack of plastic shovels laying on a wooden platform to the right of him. He picked one up from the pile and brought it to the counter.

"That all?" the woman asked.

"Can I have a pack of Marlboros as well?"

She dropped the cigarettes on the counter.

"That all?"

"Yes."

The woman made a snorting sound and sucked the phlegm from the back of her throat into her mouth. She swished it around and swallowed it.

Russ cringed.

"$14.95," she said, sucking the phlegm back up for another round.

He handed her a twenty.

"You must be the guy who parked in the Broken Wheel lot overnight. Can't park there during storms. You're lucky you wasn't towed." She handed him his change.

"Thank you. I'll remember that," he said as he grabbed the shovel and walked back outside. He rubbed his eyes as they readjusted to the glare.

"Last chance for a plow," Hank said, lighting another cigarette.

Russ smiled.

"Maybe if I can't shovel myself out."

"Good fuckin' luck," Hank said. He turned his back to Russ, stuck out his ass and farted. The two men broke into loud laughter.

Russ walked back to the parking lot with the shovel in his hand. Ashland had fallen back, effortlessly, into the clockworks of small town life, like the storm had been nothing but white dots on the television screen, a hypothetical forecast broken down into numbers, feet and inches. In the window at the Sunnyside Diner, a waitress carried two plates heaping with eggs, bacon, and hash browns to two hunters watching her ass as she bent over an empty table for a bottle of ketchup. Pickup trucks drove precariously down Route 3 with the visors down to ward off the glare. A skinny old woman placed an "Open" sign in the window at the thrift store. The shades in the dilapidated apartments were pulled up as the townies, hungover on Budweiser and bargain whiskey, walked through dirty kitchens in search of the coffee maker. The abandoned factories in the backdrop of the town were covered with a fresh layer of snow waiting to melt.

Russ looked at the horizon over the foothills of the White Mountains. Proud and silent.

When he arrived at his car, he wiped off a thick layer of snow from the windshield with his arm. He examined the interior—the empty packs of cigarettes, the discarded fast food wrappers and an old, wrinkled road map. He thought of Melanie, her warm bed, the curve of her hip, and the little boy sitting cross-legged in front of the television.

He lifted the shovel and started to dig.